SHORTSELLERS

SHORTSELLERS

Hal Barwood

investigating a society of shills

FINITE ARTS™

Shortsellers

This is a work of fiction. Selling a security short is common practice among financial institutions, and when done according to the rules, it is perfectly legal. Reporting on financial transactions is also common practice, occasionally with malign purpose. However, all story elements depicted herein are either fictional or used fictitiously. No resemblance to any real institution, government agency, enterprise, publication, person, or any of their operations is intended.

Acknowledgments . . .

Many thanks to the adventurous readers willing to explore unfinished versions of this tale: Connie Anderson & Patrick Lenihan, Jonathan & Tobias Barwood, Denis Bassett, Bob Bates, Deb & Bob Beye, Betsy & Curt Blanchard, Beverly Graves, Peggy Sadler Gross & Paul Gross, David Hanson, John & Katie Manchester, Brian Moriarty, Patricia Pizer, Peg & Don Roberts, Eva Seed, Lee Sheldon . . .

Thanks to Google, Wikipedia, and the wonderful World Wide Web for enabling the author's virtual tours through exotic locales. And thanks to Microsoft Copilot for casual research and graphic assistance.

About the Author . . .

Hal Barwood is a veteran writer and designer. You can find out all about him right here . . .

www.finitearts.com

for
Alice, Chuck, Joe, June, Linda, Ron
our group

Table of Contents

E Pluribus Unum

— seen on dollar bills

If you don't like ZZ Top, Fuck You

— seen on a bumper sticker

Part ONE

1

THURSTON CASWELL was sitting at his desk in his house at the eastern end of Lombard Street in San Francisco. A Microsoft Word document was open on his laptop. He glanced through an uphill window at nearby Coit Tower, then lowered his eyes to the laptop screen and his reflection on it, assessing himself. Thirty five years old, blue eyes behind rimless glasses, sharp nose, sandy hair parted neatly on the left side, trim beard, mouth working on something. Not exactly a heroic face, but intelligent, thoughtful, sympathetic; a face, he flattered himself to think, that suggested unseen skills. Good enough for something, anyway. He puckered his lips, blew out a bubble gum balloon and popped it. His fingers tickled the keyboard . . .

JOURNAL:

They say if you're a writer you should keep a journal, so that's what I'm doing. Writing stuff.

My family is after me, trying to pull my inheritance because I didn't join the business; well good luck, would-be mother. I owe you an education in free will, my dear.

Meanwhile, cousin Elo wants to have dinner, and we just did, when, a week ago? He's my cousin, but I have to stop and think — how does it work? My given name is Thurston, his family name is Thurston. His mother married my mother's brother. Anyway, I think that's it. Genealogy, Jesus, you know? Thing is, his side of the family is not-so-rich. That is what you get for being a serious journalist. New York Times correspondent. Nominated for a Pulitzer. Big award for reporting on the Berkeley scandal. But money? Another loan? Sure hope not.

And if that's not enough, I've got my best — make that only — wordsmith customer trying to trim my online services. What's the term for shark if your boss is a woman?

His phone warbled to signal an incoming call from his editor at WebProse, an online content supplier and his current employer.

"Rebecca Mallory . . ."

"Hey, Skip. What have you got for me?"

"Category, history: what has twenty-five pages of high-end advertising slots?"

"You're the *Jeopardy!* champ, you tell me."

"Right. The *Twenty-Five Most Dangerous Aircraft*. I sent the pages, text with images embedded. Your assistant — Kim? — she should have everything."

Mallory let out a weary sigh. "Pile on desk, rummaging, rummaging. Okay, got it, looking at your stuff — twenty-five deadliest machines with photos. Ooh, splash page and thumbnails. Wonderful shit. Terrific. Well, if the photos are PD."

"Always. U.S. Government pix, owned by us taxpayers. Got my invoice — Caswell Clicks LLC?"

"Somewhere."

"Okay, good, I don't want to chase you guys again — thirty days for this gig."

"I'll have Wally cut the check. And, um, Skip — three things: need you to do a touch-up. Jake, our in-house guy, doesn't think the Space Shuttle qualifies."

"You want a revision? The shuttle was *the most dangerous* flying machine of all time. Lost 40% of the fleet, killed a lot of astronauts."

"Skip . . ."

"Okay, at my rate."

"No can do, pardner, this is just a minor touch-up, a polish, you owe me on this."

Caswell waggled his head to shake off the absurdity.

Mallory pressed on. "Good will, on the house, keep us on your side."

"My side. Good idea."

"Oh, and number two, animal lists have a wider appeal than male-oriented tech."

"Yeah, but older people love tech, and you can get lifestyle drug ads, worth a fortune to your clients."

"Yes, Skip, true, but our clients also like feminine products for millennials."

"You mean tampons?"

"I mean wine, Airbnb, makeup, razors, perfumes, crazy chocolate, diet drinks, safe cars, and no tires."

Caswell stared out the window. "I love demographics, don't you?"

And, three, we're thinking of AI for these things going forward."

"AI? You mean, AI writes the copy?

"Yes."

"No copyright, Bex, if you do. The Library of Congress has ruled on this."

"We know, doesn't matter, who can prove anything? But, we'd like you to come up with some hot animal prompts. Deadly spiders, maybe, or smartest birds, cutest mammals."

"Wait — what's the rate?"

"Same, only a lot fewer words."

Caswell chewed on his bubble gum, blew out another enormous bubble and popped it. "Do I strike you as a dope, Bex?"

"Beg pardon?"

He peeled the bubble film off his face. "Dim, dense, dull, a useless dumbass . . ."

"Not at all, why?"

"Because it sounds like you expect me to fall for your tale of woe. Sorry, Bex, AI? Come on, that scenario doesn't really float my boat. Tell that to your chatbot overlord. I'll have to move on.

AdSpot is still human last I heard, and I think they want me."

A long pause followed while Mallory composed her response. Tactful? Blunt? Finally, blunt enough: "Understood, Skip, have a great life."

He stabbed at a button on his smartphone to kill the call. "Crap."

2

ELLIOT THURSTON pulled a chair away from a second floor table in John's Grill, a classic San Francisco bistro nested between Ellis and Market streets, and admired for its polished wood decor, its cocktails, its jazz combos, and its traditional menu. Skip Caswell slid into the offered seat, checked the cocktail menu, and ordered a Talisker whisky neat from the hovering waiter. He rubbed his fingers on the dazzling white tablecloth.

"Nice spot you picked. I needed a Lyft to get here," he complained.

"Yeah, well, I knew you'd want to pay, so I figured might as well have some good food while we chat."

"I don't want to pay," corrected Caswell. "God knows, but since you're my penniless cousin, I'm willing."

Caswell's drink arrived. They touched glasses. "Just like old times, and recent times come to think of it, namely last week."

"Yeah, I miss you."

"Feeling is mutual. How much do you need?"

"Nothing, old pal. I'm here to clear my debts, why we're celebrating in style."

"You're kidding, right?"

"Not tonight."

The waiter appeared to take their orders. Sam Spade's Lambchops for Thurston, Broiled Deluxe Burger for Caswell. A bottle of house red to share.

Thurston handed over an envelope. "Go ahead, open it."

Caswell raised his eyebrows, ran a finger under the envelope's flap, and peeked inside at five one-hundred dollar bills and a cashier's check. He whistled. "Twenty-five hundred? That's a big check for you, and another five on Ben Franklin's ticket."

"Yup, soon we'll be even." Thurston grinned. "The rest to come very soon. Unless things skid. You never know."

Caswell shook the envelope and heard a rattle. He reached inside and plucked an SD memory card half the size of a postage stamp from between the bills and held it up between thumb and forefinger.

"What's this?"

Thurston waved to dismiss it. "A memento. Secret of my life in an old photograph. Remember camping up on Simcoe Lake?"

"Sure. Those were the days."

"When you get home, pop it into your laptop, have a glimpse of our glorious past."

Caswell frowned. "Hey, Elo, what the fuck? I never knew your cynical self for sentiment. You didn't just strike it rich . . . so . . . what's up?

"You mean the money?

"For starters. Merest curiosity, you understand."

"I wrote an article."

"You write all the time. *The Chron, New York Times, the Post.*"

"And I got paid to do it."

"You mean real money, not your usual starvation wages."

"That's right."

Caswell checked the cashier's check again. He waved it at his cousin. "Tell me."

Thurston worked at his lambchops, offering an explanation between bites. *"Enterprise journalism,* Skip. Like Woodward and Bernstein, remember them? You look for some social or economic issue, maybe political corruption, and you figure out how to frame the problem, how to contact relevant sources to give your idea some gravity, and then you attack the bad guys with nasty ink."

"Mmm . . ."

"It's a real weapon. Only . . . this time I didn't scratch my left-wing liberal itch. The idea came to me."

Caswell's frown deepened. He aimed a french fry at his dinner companion. "How so . . ?"

"Some very wealthy dude — don't know who — paid me to write a hit piece about a local startup that just went through a big and hugely successful IPO."

"Unicorn kind of thing."

"Yes. A company called *VectorSafe Technology.* Well, the stock isn't moving like my guy thought, and he wants to unload a big investment, so his company — whoever that is — is shorting VST's stock."

"And your article is intended to rattle investors, force the price down, make it easy for this unnamed financial guy to recoup."

"That's right."

"Who is this guy — really?"

"Honestly, Bro, I really don't know." Thurston drained his glass. "The cash in that envelope? That's a small chunk of what came my way in that same envelope. Love it, right? The mystery . . . makes you shiver."

"Good Christ, Elo. *The New York Times* ran this piece?"

"Sure, why not?"

"No fact check? In the deepfake era, folks are usually kind of careful about stuff."

"Oh, they ran a check all right. I did my research, found several ways to denigrate VST management, all based on real research, *no problemo.*"

"So this V-S-whatever, this startup, they're pulling some kind of hyped-up fraud?"

Thurston shook his head. "Can't say that. They're naïve,

they're tone deaf. But truth is, they're as solid as newbies ever are. All the same, I did document a few angles that invite financial doubt."

"Wow. Look at you. I am in awe."

"And get this, strike two, citing VST's deeper problems, that's a fastball going to press as we speak. "

Thurston cast a nervous eye around the room. He cocked his head, gave his napkin a twirl. "I have received death threats."

Caswell clocked the mood swing. "Shit, of course you have."

"Only one, actually. I shouldn't exaggerate."

"Please don't."

Thurston opened his wallet and extracted a crinkled-up note. He passed it to Caswell, who unfolded the scrap of paper to expose two lines of text printed on someone's inkjet printer:

CEASE DESIST OR DIE
THIS MEANS YOU

Caswell sat back in his chair. "This is serious? It looks serious."

Thurston bobbed his head up and down. "Pretty cool, don't you think?"

"And article two is already in the pipeline? You could retract it. You know, 'mistakes were made'."

"Never — that would end my career. I'd wind up writing ads for Safeway. Besides, I don't give a damn."

"Holy hotdogs, cousin, watch your ass."

"I'll be all right."

"You don't look too sure about that. My advice? Lock your door. Get a gun. Fucking learn how to shoot."

3

HOBART BUTTERFIELD, VectorSafe Technology's chief financial officer, was jogging on an interactive cardio trainer in VectorSafe's twelfth floor workout room, nursing a hangover. He gazed at a spectacular view of San Francisco Bay through a wide north-facing window while he ran. A fog-free morning let him pick out Alcatraz and the long white wakes of Golden Gate ferries on the move. The sight warmed him, confirming his choice of expensive offices for the new company. On the screen attached to his treadmill lush green countryside was flowing past. He was in a virtual half-marathon in northern Germany with thirty other runners. His position, recently as high as fifth, was now eroding while he sipped a latte from nearby Starbucks. He didn't seem to mind.

Randal Butterfield, VectorSafe CEO, Hobie's father, and co-founder of the company they jointly managed, rolled a $10,000 Trek road bike into the room, hooked it up on a wall, wove a braided steel cable through the wheels and frame, and locked it in place.

"Whoa, Dad, we're in our own office. Who's going to steal your bike?"

"No one, that's who. I love this bike."

"Who could tell?"

The elder Butterfield scowled. "I know where we are. I know the odds. I know our people. But . . . gotta be vigilant, son. Always vigilant."

The younger Butterfield let his cadence wind down. He stepped away from his machine and handed Dad a latte.

"Sorry, getting cold now. I thought you'd be here already."

"Beautiful morning, I took the long way in." He picked up a towel, wiped his face and arms, muscled himself onto a high bench. He swirled the coffee in its paper cup.

"You see today's *Times?*"

"You mean the shooting in Memphis? The plane that crashed into Mammoth Mountain?"

Dad lifted his eyes toward heaven. "Good God, my CFO's an idiot. Living proof that nepotism is overrated."

"Come on, Dad — I read. I just thought we should start the fight with some good news. Those incidents show us a market for our products."

"Forget all that sentimental TV fodder. Hey, shit happens. I'm talking tragedy. Ours."

"What?"

"Our stock price, wavering for a couple of weeks, and now dropping."

"Take it easy, no heart attack, okay? We'll bounce back."

"Wake up, son. We're down because someone is pushing us down. *Shorting us.* Who? Don't know. Ackman? Icahn? Peltz? The real question is how? How is he doing it?

"Yeah, how — I can see you've been thinking again."

"It's that article in *The Times.* Reprinted on Motley Fool, retailed on ten podcasts, telling everyone how our products don't work, won't ship, violate patents, and hinting that sexual harassment charges are pending."

"Oh that: who believes that shit?"

"Well now . . . just about any investor with a shred of sanity."

"Come on, old man — we are golden, pulling the economy into the fucking future by the scruff of its neck. Hey, look north — we can see X and Uber headquarters, up on Market. And know what? We're taller than they are. We are looking down on them."

Dad crossed his arms.

"Listen up, Chief. Our IPO went through the roof. The elixir of AI worked its magic. But the truth is, our products are facing a recall. Bugs in the software, possible defective chips. Talk to Marvin of Finn & Quimby? We've got a patent suit on our hands for the navigation algorithms. And . . . to top it off, Edie May quit last week. Shook a finger at me and left."

The color drained from Hobie's face.

"Whoa there, Dad, don't tell me you *touched* her?"

Dad shrugged. "I may have brushed a hand across her butt when we were heading back from lunch."

"Lunch? Butt? Oh. My. God. What would Mom say? What will Edie May's *lawyer* say?"

"Your mother has been out of the picture for a long time, Hobie. She says nothing."

Hobie reached toward his father with earnest advice. "So you get deposed, you can't remember, you deny that gold digger's claim all the way."

Dad made a peevish face.

"Let's stay on target here — Rod's an optimist down on the factory floor, but he knows we will not be able to bring all our stuff to market without an infusion of capital. Do we take a loan? From who? Reading this stuff, financial folks are going to be very nervous.

"We need to issue a new round of stock. Who will invest if this corporate assassination attempt goes any further? The stock market is not annoyed with VST, it is fucking furious."

Hobie drank the last drop of his latte, took aim at a waste basket twenty feet away and arched a shot that sank his cup without popping the lid. "He shoots, he scores. So, what do we do?"

Dad opened a saddlebag on his bike, shook open a three-day-old paper edition of *The New York Times* and jabbed a finger at the business page:

VECTORSAFE OR VECTORSCAM?

"That article has an author. Find out who's paying him. Discourage him from any follow-up. Do it before some other nut is paid to hack us and the cops find porn on our corporate network."

Hobie picked up a kettle ball and hefted it high. "You mean, 'who will rid me of this turbulent priest?'"

Dad turned to go, clattering away on his bike cleats. "I didn't say that. As for Edie May? If worse comes to worst, I'll marry her." He grinned. "Do a pre-nup with generous terms."

▼

In his office, having showered and dressed, the younger Butterfield turned to his phone.

"Hunter Investments. How may I direct your call?"

"Speak to Dan Leavitt, please."

While he waited for the call to connect he selected a tie from his desk drawer and tied a four-in-hand, using his office window as a mirror.

"This is Leavitt. Hobie? What's new?"

"That's my question for you. You guys are holding our stock."

Leavitt cleared his throat. "Yes we are. You know, we're big fans of VST, love your ideas, your energy . . . but . . ."

"But what? We're good, right? On our way up together."

"I dunno, Hobe — you saw *The Times* piece? — it's giving us the jitters. Sleepless nights."

"Come on, *The Times?* What do they know?"

"Maybe nothing, but that guy Thurston, the writer, he's obviously shilling for a hedge fund who wants you dead and thinks you're an easy kill."

"We're not. We're solid. Your investment is going to go through the roof, and we're very grateful for your faith in us."

"We are hoping."

"Now we've got revolutionary products we're set to deliver, but it looks like the push to market and profitability will require a new round of paper. Can we count on Hunter?"

Leavitt suppressed a cough. "I like your style, Hobie. It's good to be aggressive. But I have to say our financial analysts have your light burning yellow. Wait and see."

"Really? We need this to rev up production, and you need this to see what I promise will be a handsome return."

"Sorry, Hobie. We're going to watch the kettle. If and when it starts to boil again, call me."

Butterfield propped his arms on his desk, lowered his head into his hands.

"And Hobie? Let's hope we don't see any more *Times* hit pieces. Very bad for business."

Butterfield killed the call, punched the number for Belknap Wealth Management.

"Yeah, we're still on board. Attenuating our position, though. Nice and slow, no ripples, I guess you'd say. Sucks, but that's life on the firing line."

Butterfield surveyed a list on his laptop, silently weighed the prospects, and dialed up Megatrend Equities.

"VST? Have you lost your fucking mind?"

Butterfield ran a finger over his list. Aha! Good old Prosperity Global Partners, always an ally.

"Shit on toast, Butterfield. Essential personnel quitting? Defaulting loans? Illegal aliens running your plant? Software bugs? Little kids firing your so-called safe guns?"

Butterfield took a deep breath. "Hey, Phil, that's all crap. Move along, nothing to see there."

"Oh yeah? It's all laid out in this morning's *Times.* Take two. Didn't you see it?"

Butterfield stood up from his desk and stumbled out into the office pool. His face was gray. He leaned over the rim of his assistant's cubicle.

"Hi, Jane. Need a copy of today's *Times.* Paper edition, confirm what I'm reading online. Then call Marvin over at Finn & Quimby to make room for me this morning."

"Subject of discussion?"

"Solve a financial problem."

"Sounds serious."

"It is. And bring me a triple latte with extra Tylenol."

4

TRAFFIC at 7:00 PM in San Francisco's North Beach district was crawling homeward along Columbus Avenue, bumper to bumper in both directions. Drivers with frayed tempers were honking and swerving to get out of the way of a northbound AMR ambulance using its godawful siren to bully through the sheet metal crush. At the southwest corner of Washington Square park it veered onto Union Street and pulled to the curb. Emergency medical technicians in full battle dress, a man and a woman, leaped from the vehicle.

"What do you see?"

"Nada."

Light was fading, so they swept the area with powerful flashlights. The woman's beam lit up a pair of shoes. She pointed.

"Here."

Lying among low bushes and partially hidden in the shadow of a park bench was a splayed-out figure. The EMTs pulled on nitrile gloves and stooped for a closer look.

"Male, middle thirties. Clean shaven. Dark hair. Casual dress. Eyes look closed. Um, definitely closed."

The woman readied an oxygen tank. They knelt down, composed the man's arms and legs. The woman applied oxygen while her partner checked for a pulse. They kept at it for five minutes.

"O-2 is empty. Do we call it?"

"Yes, gotta call it — this guy is D-R-T, on his way to heaven."

Alerted by the siren, a well-knit man wearing a Giants warmup jacket emerged from an apartment building across the street to watch the medical emergency unfold. When the EMTs stood up from their unsuccessful labors, he moved purposely toward the park, thrusting out his arms to deter impatient commuters while he deftly maneuvered between their automobiles.

"Hello there, troopers," he said.

The EMTs swiveled around. "Say what?"

The man, of Asian heritage, held up an ID card with a badge attached. The EMTs aimed flashlights at it.

The man raised a hand to shield his eyes against the glare. "Dennis Yao. Police inspector. I was hunting for brass from our latest gang war over there, not getting very far, and this looked more interesting."

He thumbed the voice recorder on his smartphone and turned it toward the pair. "So what's going on?"

The male EMT toed the body's leg. "Got a fatality here."

"Foul play?"

"Nah, no wounds, no bruises, no defensive cuts. Heart attack at a guess."

Your names?"

They looked at each other.

"I'm Pete Black," said the man.

"Pat White," said the woman.

"You're kidding."

"It's okay. People call us the Panda Twins."

Yao nodded. He stooped to inspect the body while dictating his impressions.

"Ah, 7:20 PM, southwest corner Washington Square, I am here in the presence of two AMR EMTs, Pete and Pat — the Panda Twins, gotta love that — and a corpse. Male, dressed casually, approximately thirty-five years, guessing well-housed, no obvious cause of death evident."

He stood up.

"Was he breathing when you found him?"

"No, Sir."

"Did you attempt to revive him?"

"That's the drill."

"Of course you did. How were you dispatched?"

Pete gestured toward invisible cell towers. "Got a call."

"Anything look funny to you guys?"

Pat grimaced. "You'd think. But no, this happens all the time."

"Need a name, but that can wait for forensics."

Pete reached into a pocket and sheepishly offered up two small items. "There's this stuff. Found it lying beside the body. Man's wallet and his old-time phone."

"You take a look?"

"You got here first. So no."

"Well, I will call this in. I notice his arms and legs have been rearranged. Don't touch the body again, okay? This is a possible crime scene and forensics will want a clean look."

"Got it."

Yao zipped up his jacket.

"Then good night, and thanks for being professional."

He turned and walked back toward Columbus, then paused before crossing to remove a California driver license from the dead man's wallet.

"Here's an ID for you two. Now your body isn't just a random corpse. He's a person. Was, anyway . . ."

Pat cupped a hand around her ear to encourage the punch line.

". . . some guy named Elliot Thurston."

5

SKIP CASWELL was up early, lounging in sweat pants, a 49ers sweat shirt, and Nike running shoes. He cradled a cup of fresh-squeezed orange juice while he made the rounds of his small house, savoring his narrow views of the city outside.

A casual inspection of his pantry revealed a serious lack of backup food. No cookies. No Perrier. No multivitamins. He checked his refrigerator. Bare. No sliced cheese. No emergency lasagna.

"Damn."

What else? He checked his printer. Ink very low, and stupidly expensive at his local office supply store. Gotta face it, time for Costco.

Caswell considered taking the bus, but the likely bulk his list would generate caused him to drive his 2010 Space Gray Metallic BMW M3 Coupe across the city to 11th and Divisidero, where he cautiously rolled into Costco's gigantic parking structure. There he eased up the ramp to the roof and backed into a safe corner spot next to the exit stairs.

He flashed his membership card to the troll guarding the store entrance and found himself walking under a colorfully decorated cardboard arch into a world of tropical splendor made out of paper. A young salesman stood in his way.

"Tom Shay here, glad I caught your eye. Take a moment, Sir. I represent MyWorld Experiences, and have I got a deal for you."

Caswell looked around. He sidestepped. The salesman did the same: a dance of commerce.

"A deal? Hot tubs? Rain gutters?"

"Nothing so ordinary. Partnering with everyone's favorite Big

Box, we're offering vacations."

"Beach in Hawaii?"

"Better than that. Sign up with us, you won't own a location, nothing that ties you down to a single place. No danger of boredom. You will own actual vacations all over the world."

Caswell regarded the decorations.

"I am impressed with the presentation."

"Glad you recognize the potential, Sir."

"And Costco let you set up in here?"

"Of course, we're partners."

"Probably cost you, not them, I guess."

"We are mutual beneficiaries, for sure, and I'm thinking you're just the man to share it all with us."

"Timeshare, right? You're selling timeshares."

"We don't use that term, no."

Caswell felt just annoyed enough to push the conversation forward.

"Tell me, you're pretty young, look new. Have you been to all these resorts?"

"Not all, but I do enjoy the perks. You will too."

"I dunno. I'm worried."

"How so?"

"Well, I didn't think I looked gullible, but maybe I do. Timeshares — why would I ever? You're trying to stick me with a tar baby of the leisure world."

Caswell shot out a hand to squelch the eager young salesman's rebuttal. His phone was buzzing. He noted the caller's name.

"Sorry, have fun in Acapulco." He lifted his phone. "Gotta take this call."

He turned away and stationed himself in a quiet corner near the tires on display.

"Mamie? Skip. Nice to hear your voice. How are you?"

His caller sniffled and blew her nose.

"Mamie? You okay?"

"Did you . . . hear the news?"

The voice was throaty. Caswell pictured tears flowing.

"What news, Mamie?"

"Elo."

▼

On a brisk day in late September, the entire Thurston and Caswell families, not known for socializing together, gathered at the San Francisco ferry terminal.

"Whose idea was this?"

"Skip, I think. Or Mamie. They talked it over."

When the entire clan was finally assembled, they boarded Golden Gate ferry *MV Napa* for a maritime excursion to celebrate the life of Elliot Thurston, recently departed.

Representing the bereaved Thurston family, Elliot's father Louis and his mother Mamie crossed the gangway and took up positions on the lower stern deck. Thurston Caswell, mildly peeved by the confusion his formal name would cause in this company, followed close behind. He was trailed by his father Robert Senior, his fifty-year-old stepmother Bella, and Robert Junior, his older brother.

They were joined by a crush of strangers and out-of-town tourists eager for a taste of salt air. At the last minute, as one of the deckhands was preparing to stow the gangway, a red-haired woman in a wool coat skipped aboard.

Gas turbines howled, the deck shuddered, and the boat's thrusters shoved it away from the terminal. Out on the open water of San Francisco Bay the ferry, a twin-hulled catamaran, accelerated sharply. The passengers staggered and jostled each other.

Not many among them were interested in their destination, Vallejo on the north shore of San Pablo Bay. They just wanted to feel a blast of wind in their hair as the boat sliced through the waves at forty knots.

Robert Senior reached into a shoulder bag and withdrew a magnum of chardonnay. Robert Junior fetched plastic wine glasses from a jacket pocket. Mamie Thurston opened a picnic box revealing half a dozen cylindrical cardboard cartons. Louis poured wine and they all lifted their glasses.

"Here's to Elo," said his father.

"To Elo!" chorused the family.

The red-haired woman who boarded at the last minute hovered nearby, but did not approach. A ferry steward watching the ceremony, however, elbowed his way into their midst.

"What's going on here?" he demanded.

"We're celebrating," said Mamie.

"What's in that box, Ma'am?"

"Our only son's ashes, if you must know."

"We're going to scatter them on the bay," explained Bella.

"Hey, hey, hey — no you're not. This isn't a funeral parlor, you can't use public transport for that. It's illegal."

Robert Junior was an attorney. "You sure about that? The statute? Got it handy?"

The steward scowled. "No, but we run a clean ship. It's against policy."

"Oh really," said Bella, biting off the words. "You want to prosecute a grieving family? Or maybe just go about your duties instead? Huh? Please ignore us, we're very clean."

The steward stood in place for a moment, thinking things over. Then he made a little salute. "Go ahead, enjoy the day," he decided and marched away.

As Louis Thurston began a celebration speech, Robert Senior refilled his younger son's glass. "Drink up. Here's to the future."

"Mud in your eye," said Skip.

"You know, laddie, you don't have to lurk around the edges of our company, you could take your place with the rest of us."

Skip allowed a faint and faintly worrisome curiosity to take hold. "What would I be doing? I'm no attorney. I write reams of worthless clickbait for low rent websites."

His father considered this. "I'm not talking about our flagship office complexes up and down the coast. That takes expertise you don't have."

"Nope, sure don't."

"Hear me out — we also own three golf courses in the Bay Area, and one up in Bend, Oregon. You could run them."

"I don't play golf."

This response triggered a spark of irritation in the old man; made his eye twitch.

"Well then," he wondered, "what are you good for?"

Skip winced. "Not much, I guess."

He pointed toward Elo's father who was opening the box of ashes. "Here we go, Dad, let's pay attention."

"Ashes to ashes, we're told," mumbled the elder Thurston. His eyes were clouding over "My son, gone too soon," he gurgled, "now returning to the great mother of us all, the Sea and the Earth itself."

The family members took ash cartons in hand, ripped the tops free and shook streams of white powder over the ferry's stern.

The red-haired woman hanging around had now retired to the upper deck. She looked down upon the gathering as Mamie Thurston shook a handful of rose petals onto the water.

Skip turned to face them all. "Elo was my cousin, but more than that, he was my best friend. He won the FJ dinghy sailing trophy in college — why we're out here freezing our asses on a boat today, right? He was a serious award-winning journalist, a wine expert, Giants fan win or lose, social justice champ, tireless explainer of current events, and a decent poker player. But most important, he was an honorable and cheerful man whose only fault was the money he owed me."

The family chuckled politely.

"And now he doesn't owe anybody anything." Skip waved and stepped back into the group, all of them staring at the ferry's wake and the ash cloud whirling away.

▼

Halfway back on the return trip, as the ferry skirted Alcatraz, Skip observed the red-haired woman pluck yellow petals from the flowers of a small bouquet she had brought aboard and, following Mamie Thurston's example, fling them over the stern.

On the dock in San Francisco, Skip gave Elo's mom a big parting hug. From the corner of an eye he noticed the red-haired woman disembarking. She walked away without a word.

"Hey, Mame, you recognize her?"

"You mean the redhead? Yeah, I saw her. Elo's special friend?"

"Could be. Kind of shy, though, don't you think?"

6

BOB'S BAVARIAN BARBERSHOP on Columbus Avenue, less than half a mile downhill from Skip Caswell's house, looked like it might have once been the real thing. It even had a barber pole hanging outside with red and blue bands spiraling eternally upward.

The wide roll-up door was a giveaway, however, and the interior setup did not include barber chairs. Three different BMW automobiles were up on hydraulic lifts while mechanics inspected their brake lines and changed their oil.

Caswell's M3 Coupe was one of the Beamers. He and Bob himself, a man in his forties wearing an immaculate gray coverall, were discussing its problems.

"When you punch it? What's the response?"

Caswell framed the situation by scratching his head. "I dunno. Slow. We don't accelerate the way we should."

"There. That's it. The symptom, plain as day."

"Oh?"

Caswell had learned to trust Bob's work after many visits over a number of years. Now his ripoff antenna was starting to vibrate.

"We'll clean your fuel jets, change the oil, etc. Transmission fluid is out of date, by the way, as well."

"Hmm, sounds like a doctor visit."

"But that's not your real problem. Your baby Beamer needs a new Engine Control Unit."

Caswell, a man with money in the bank, nevertheless paled at the thought.

"Whoa, a computer. What's that going to cost me?"

As Caswell stared blankly at his service rep he formed the

impression that the coveralls on Bob were there to disguise someone with a business degree from UCLA or Berkeley instead of a diploma from a life in greasy maintenance pits.

"That part — we'll have to get on the horn to locate new old stock, you understand — is eight hundred to twelve hundred, depending."

"Depending?"

"What we find. BMW does not make computer replacements for your vehicle anymore."

"Holy shit, this is ridiculous. What am I staring at?"

Bob gestured toward the wounded Beamer. "Together with your routine maintenance, right around twenty-five hundred. I'll write you up to nail that number down."

Caswell stuffed his hands in his pockets. "Supposing you find a working computer on a wreck. Let's try that. And let's wait on the fuel jets for another day."

Bob's demeanor stiffened. His voice hardened. "You'll be making a big mistake, my friend. Your ride and I have been through a lot together. Be a shame to skimp and let her go downhill."

Caswell didn't know whether he really needed a new computer or not. He was sure Bob was taking advantage of his profound automotive ignorance, however, and he wanted to show some spine.

"All right. I don't mind spending money when I have to, but I don't like getting clipped. So let's do the routine stuff, and call me when you've got something off some maniac's total that won't set me back my entire 401k."

Bob locked his hands around an imaginary rope. "You the man, Skip. Just remember, when you need a tow" — he tugged — "make sure it's on a flatbed."

▼

Feeling mighty glum about his fellow citizens, Caswell plodded southeast on Columbus, heading for the bus stop. He was lost in thought and failed to notice a red-haired woman watching him from across the street.

The bus arrived and Caswell swung aboard. He took a seat halfway back and opened his phone to check for messages. He didn't look up when the red-haired woman came down the aisle and found a seat a few rows behind.

He rode four blocks and stepped off at Union Street. There he crossed over to the southwest corner of Washington Square park. He had an itch to see exactly where cousin Elo breathed his last and wanted to scratch it.

What he saw on a cool morning were neatly kept grounds planted with decorative bushes and small trees, a relief from the buildings crowding Columbus. He felt no supernatural vibes, saw nothing to indicate a recent untimely death. Benches set out here and there invited strollers to slow down and relax. Caswell took the hint and sat down facing into the park where kids were running back and forth, attempting to launch little kites.

"Heart attack, Elo? At your age. My age too, but I feel fine. Should feel fine, anyway. Life — no guarantees on the product, huh? No returns and your money back, what little you actually had."

He stood up, and ambled over to the kids. As a kite wobbled by, he reached out and grabbed it.

"Can I try?"

"Who are you, Mister?"

"I live up the street here." He pointed. "Your problem is altitude. Got to get this puppy up where we have some wind."

He gave the kite line a series of sharp jerks, letting it run through his fingers between pulls. Soon the little tissue paper square was floating serenely above the trees in a light breeze.

"Oooh," said the owner, "we're flying!"

Caswell handed him the line. "Have fun while you're out here. It's important."

Caswell turned up his jacket collar against the morning chill and resumed walking southeast. The red-haired woman watched him go from the Union Street bus stop.

At Stockton Street he recrossed Columbus and was shown to a table inside Caffè Pappardelle, his favorite Italian restaurant in San Francisco's most Italian neighborhood.

The waiter made a little bow. "What are we having this morning, Skip? Besides a latte."

Caswell ordered a frittata and opened his phone to pass the inevitable wait time on his Kindle app. Within a couple of minutes his downcast eyes caught purple running shoes attached to bare ankles closing in. He straightened up.

The red-haired woman backed into a chair and sat down facing him. She rested her elbows on the table.

Caswell's eyebrows ratcheted up a notch. Before either could speak, the waiter arrived with Caswell's frittata.

"Say, Jack, my brunch companion just arrived. Could you put my dish in a warm-up oven and bring it back with something for her?"

"Sure. What can I get you, Ma'am?"

The red-haired woman tilted her head. "The frittata looks nice."

Caswell pointed. "That and something sweet. She needs the pickup, did a long walk this morning."

The waiter hurried away with the order.

"Well," said the red-haired woman, "that was nicely done. Very smooth."

Caswell ran a finger past his eyes. "Don't give me too much credit. I didn't spot you."

"Ah, playing to the crowd."

"I haven't been here with a woman since Veronica left me high and dry. Jack is going to make assumptions. Your arrival will power the kitchen gossip here for a week."

"I see. Elliot said you were kind of a loner."

Caswell turned off his phone. He studied the woman. Her freckled face made him think the red hair was natural. Her eyes were green, her gaze intense. Her voice was a contralto hum with a light accent that might have come from Boston.

"You have a name, I hope?"

"Azalea Prudhomme. Call me Sally."

"You knew Elo."

"Yes."

"How well?"

She put on a modest smile. "Well enough."

Brunch arrived. She took a bite of her frittata.

"Mmm, this is good." She touched her napkin to her lips. "And now that we've met, Thurston, I can say I know you."

Caswell reached across the table, and they shook hands.

"Mystery solved. Glad you decided to come out of the woodwork. Everyone was wondering."

She made an apologetic little bow. "Elliot never introduced me to anyone in your families. I wanted to get an impression, understand if I was going to be shunned or resented."

"Don't worry about it. By the way, it's 'Skip.' Nobody calls me 'Thurston.'"

"Here's the deal, Skip. The reason I've been following you people around the town."

She paused to collect herself.

"Category, death, and here's the clue: this method of leaving Earth doesn't use rockets."

Caswell couldn't help himself. "What is murder?" he blurted.

"That is correct. Elliot didn't die of a heart attack. He was murdered."

Caswell blinked. "You heard about my quiz show career."

"Of course. Your cousin told me all about you."

"But, whoa there, *Jeopardy!* is not a crime show."

"I know this is coming out of nowhere, but I've got an argument for my idea. Will you hear it?"

"An argument — what is it you do for a living, Miss — sorry — make that *Sally.*"

She presented her business card:

SPOT ON SPOTS
Commercials and Product Placement
Hit home runs on TV with Sally P

"I'm a TV commercial producer. Local ads mostly. I write copy for magazines now and then."

"Must be fun."

"Work is hell, but I love what I do."

Caswell tapped his forehead. "The penny drops — you're Elo's girlfriend.

"Sort of. Elliot was a funny guy. We didn't live together."

"Not ready to pop the question, I take it."

"But he was in the peak of health. There were threats."

"I know, he showed me one. But murder? Fatal heart attacks can sneak up on people. It's famous."

Prudhomme removed two sheets of paper from her bag and handed them over. "Recent medical tests."

Caswell read the results. "Blood panel normal on three, four, fifteen lines of evidence. Cholesterol? Lower than the soles of my shoes. EKG shows his heart pumping away like new." He sighed. "Good God, woman . . ."

A momentary shadow crossed his face.

"Bereavement, it's understandable, but the EMTs were right there. He dropped dead."

Prudhomme shook her head. "Elliot was an investigative reporter. Risky work, you agree?"

"I dunno. We're not in a movie."

Prudhomme pointed an accusing finger.

"I understand you dabble in journalism yourself. Maybe it's hard to see professional danger while writing listicles and shaggy dog stories for marginal ad-starved websites."

Caswell was not embarrassed. "Got me. I am an idler."

"You have money."

"I'm comfortable."

"Wealth is a drug to keep reality out of focus," she declared, fisting the table for emphasis. "But I watched you check out the spot where he died just now, so I know you're concerned."

"Sue me for being curious."

Prudhomme's cheeks were starting to burn.

"Come on, *Skip,* where's your sense of outrage? Where's your ambition? You should look into this, the police have got it all wrong. Somebody didn't like my pal and what he was up to, exposing a shitty company that's fooling its stockholders."

Caswell leaned back to lessen the verbal blows. He re-read her medical reports.

"This" — he rattled the pages — is pretty thin stuff. You're so hot, become a detective. You could be Miss Marple, take two."

"I'm trying. You're my first case."

7

INSPECTOR DENNIS YAO was leaning over a desk in the third floor war room of the San Francisco Police Department's Central Station, located on Vallejo Street just off Columbus. He was shuffling papers, looking for anything that might shed light on the latest gang shootout he was working. However, the testimony of gang members as reported by their interviewers in uniform was inconclusive, as was the ballistics report from forensics.

The duty officer poked his head into the room. "Hey, Dino — got somebody wants to see you."

"What about?"

"That guy who fell over in Washington Square."

Yao rolled his eyes.

"A witness? A relative? Better be one or the other."

"Family . . . a cousin, he said."

Yao blew out a sigh. "Okay, bring him in."

The duty officer stood aside and Skip Caswell appeared. He was carrying a manila folder with papers inside. He crossed the room and introduced himself.

"Hello, my name is Skip Caswell, I'm Elliot Thurston's cousin. The guy who died in the park."

Yao offered his hand and they shook. "Right. I happened to be nearby when the EMT's arrived and did a brief investigation."

"I read the report. I just thought I should follow up — give some comfort to the family."

"Sure, I understand. The EMTs on the case are solid pros, and they determined that your cousin died of natural causes, presumably a heart attack. Unusual for a man of his age, but it does happen."

Caswell waved his manila folder. "I've got something here I'd like to show you."

Yao made a come-along gesture and led the way to his office, a small alcove off the war room. There he reoccupied his chair and held out his arm for the folder.

Caswell took a seat on the hard wooden visitor's chair to watch him check out the material.

Yao donned a pair of reading glasses and silently leafed through the papers, turning each sheet over as he skimmed the contents. After a couple minutes of studious attention he looked up.

"The medical reports. How recent?"

"See the date on there? Two months."

"He certainly appears to be in the best of health."

"I had dinner with him a few days before he passed. That's my impression, for sure."

Yao held up the printed threat.

"This real? It's not hand-written, just an ink-jet printout on ordinary paper, so no possible forensics. From my point of view, could be a prank. Where'd you get it?"

"Elo's effects. I'm his personal rep. He kept it in his wallet and showed it to me at our dinner. He didn't think it was a joke. What a dope — he was proud of getting it. A badge of honor."

"No date?"

"Nope."

Yao rustled the newsprint. "And here we have an article in *The New York Times*. I see the byline. That belong to your cousin?"

"Of course. He was a serious journalist. Freelance, but published in papers and magazines up and down the coast and all over the country."

"Got it. Well, tell your family to love each other, and please give them my condolences on your cousin's untimely passing."

'I will," said Caswell. He paused. "But that's not really why I wanted to see you."

Yao smiled. "I didn't really think so. You suspect foul play. Murder."

"Elo's girlfriend suspects, and I thought she was just having trouble coping. But she got me thinking. Now I wonder if someone working at the target company of Elo's articles had it in for him."

Yao re-read the lead paragraph. "VectorSafe Technology. Who's that?"

Caswell opened his arms to encompass total ignorance.

Yao reached onto a shelf behind his desk for a different folder. He extracted a photo of Elliot Thurston's left arm. "Have a look at this . . ."

Caswell noticed bruising and a prominent puncture mark.

Yao tapped the mark. "Got a track here. Maybe your cousin wasn't really in the best of health after all."

Caswell was offended. "Elo would never do drugs. Never. Caffeine enough to wash him away, a beer and a glass of wine, but that's it."

Yao moved to pick up the photo.

"Hey wait, let me see that."

Yao shoved it across his desktop.

Caswell examined the arm, its bruises, and the puncture mark.

"That hole. Kind of big, I'd say. Does that look like a needle track to you?"

Yao waved dismissively. "What else? I'm guessing the man was new at it, sloppy. I see you're shocked, but people have secrets, even from their families, you know?"

Caswell sensed a creeping uncertainty in the detective. "I've got another question. How did the EMT's get there? Who called them in?"

Yao let out a sigh. He opened the police report to check. "Call was made from his phone."

Caswell tugged at the report. "May I?"

Yao handed it over.

"All right, look here. Elo was dead when the EMT's got there. How do you know Elo made the call? Maybe the killer, if Elo was killed, wanted him found. I dunno, deter someone else?'

Yao put up his hands to fend off the idea. "Big if."

"Did you get prints off the phone?"

Yao squirmed. Here comes this amateur, and he landed on a pro's rare mistake.

"We did not."

Caswell pressed on. "I'm surprised. Might be important."

Yao stood up. "Thanks for coming in, sharing your concerns. But the investigation is closed. The medical examiner has ruled natural causes, and that's that. We move on."

Caswell wasn't satisfied. "I was all set to do exactly that" — he scowled — "but you know, now I'm not."

Yao motioned toward the door. "Tell you what, Mr. Caswell, I'll get some prints off that phone for you."

He placed a hand on Caswell's shoulder and guided him firmly out of his office.

"Whatever it takes to ease your mind."

8

AT HOME IN HIS OFFICE, Skip Caswell was brooding over life's odd turns:

JOURNAL:

So here's the thing — Elo's death. It all points to heart failure, and I see the evidence, but I just met Elo's girlfriend. Sally. Well, sometime girlfriend anyway, says she's a TV producer. I couldn't quite grok the relationship they had, how it worked. Were they in love? Hard to tell, but she sure is on a galloping high horse claiming Elo was f-ing murdered. Why? His NYT hit pieces. And even though it looked like you could buy the thing on Amazon, I did see a threat note he claimed to get.

I would like to leave this crap behind — Elo, his fate (if that's what it was), Elo's pal Sally, the whole damn thing. But . . . now I'm wondering, and inspector Yao didn't say anything that will help me sleep tonight.

Caswell considered adding other thoughts, but couldn't focus on any, so he changed his mind, closed his text file, and turned to other pressing matters, his online wordsmithing career.

"What happened, AdSpot? You were supposed to keep that human touch."

Like his former employer, his new one was shifting to artificial intelligence work, something he viewed as a betrayal of the human race. He found the strange entity's name, *AdBoy,* especially grating, so much so that an old habit of talking to himself returned in force.

"Okay, Addie old Boy, I've got a lot of scrolling inches to write, so tell me, what are the world's *Twenty-Five Most Annoying Pests* — aside from you?"

Within ten seconds he had a list.

"Cockroaches reign on top, okay; followed by sugar ants;

followed by yellowjackets; followed by clothes moths; followed by bedbugs; followed by mice; followed by . . . *you.* Wow, the robot has a sense of humor. Spook-ayy!"

He typed in another prompt.

"Now, what about the world's *Twenty-Five Most Glamorous Lipstick Colors?"*

He observed a very brief pause, and a new list appeared.

"Flaming Libido from Actuelle; followed by *Tornado Red* from Beau Knot; followed by *Classified Pink* from Executrix; followed by . . . . . . my God this is boring."

He sat back. His mind was rebelling against workaday tedium by forcing his attention to the much more intriguing questions hovering around his cousin's early death. He tapped his fingers on his desktop.

"Wait a minute, what about . . . hey AdBoy, can you show me surveillance camera positions around Washington Square Park?"

"In what city, Skip?" queried the AI creature. "I see parks of that name in New York City, Philadelphia, Portland Oregon, and San Francisco. Do you have a preference?"

The hair on Caswell's neck rose. He was new to conversations like this, and the experience seemed uncanny.

"Um, San Francisco, please."

A map popped up with highlights on three spots.

"I like the one looking northwest. Show me video from three weeks ago."

"I'm sorry, Skip, I can't do that."

"What? You sound like Hal from *Space Odyssey."*

"2001 A Space Odyssey is an excellent movie, one of Stanley Kubrick's best, do you agree?"

"Forget the movie, I just want video from that camera."

"And I can't show it to you. The camera is privately owned, I do not have access, and the laws of privacy —"

"—Screw the laws. Who is allowed to see stuff?"

"Building owners. The police. Hackers."

"A lot of help you are."

Caswell switched into his email app. He was greeted by the usual throwaway messages from the Democratic Party; from Stanford, his alma mater; from the American Cancer Society; and from Job Max, a recruiting firm. He scrolled down to a note from GoFundMe, an obvious scam. Something in the text's wordage, composed in colloquial American English, made him think the message came from a sender in the United States instead of the usual suspects in India or Russia or Nigeria.

HELP ME PAY FOR COLLEGE
I'm a straight-A student hoping for a good future. I've been accepted at San Francisco State, but I can't pay the bills.
Pay it forward: your money won't be wasted.

Mildly curious, he moved the message into his spam folder where its internet links could do no harm and examined the details. Sure enough, he recognized the presence of a well-known malware loader named *Talon*.

"Oh-ho," he muttered. "Yesterday's code. A scam this clumsy means a kid is at work. Says he needs help, blah blah blah, and maybe he really does. But this is a no-no."

He noted the sender's undisguised contact list.

"Look at that. If Inspector Yao saw what I see, he'd have your ass in five minutes."

Caswell spent a moment mulling the sender's appealing naïveté. Then he sat up straight in his chair and turned back to the odious AdBoy program.

"Addie, my man, I've got a scam here some hacker sent. American, probably in the Bay Area. Can you find this person?"

"That depends, Skip, on what information you can supply."

"How about a name and an email address?"

He typed them in.

AdBoy spent more than a minute searching for an answer. The app let Caswell know of its tough task by writing a useless update on Caswell's laptop screen every ten seconds:

```
working
working
working
working
working
working
```

Then, seemingly plucked from outer space, came this response: "Sorry about the wait, Skip. The name you want is Axel Karlstrom, male, eighteen. He lives with his parents at 565 Hearst Avenue, San Francisco, 94112. Here's a map."

▼

Caswell arrived at 565 Hearst Avenue on a Lyft ride. The woman driving took time to fully explain the concept of tips, which irritated Caswell so much it almost cost her the loss of a rating star.

He stood at the curb and inspected the Karlstrom home, a modest two story building covered in beige stucco, one of hundreds of "Sunset Specials" from San Francisco's growth spurt following World War II. It resembled its neighbors but was not as well kept. The stucco was crumbling away in patches. Paint on the window frames was peeling. A few of the red tiles edging the roof had fallen off. An older Ford Econoline van was parked in the drive. Caswell registered the *Karlstrom Kleans Karpets* logo on its flanks. He swiftly tagged the house as a rental, the despair of its neighbors, and the cleaning business as more hope than comfort. No wonder the Karlstrom kid needed help.

He crossed the street and mounted a steep flight of stairs to the second-floor front door and knocked.

No response.

The grinding sound of the garage door yawning open turned him around in time to see the back of a youth pushing a beat-up mountain bike inside.

"Hello . . ?"

No answer.

Caswell knocked on the door again. He waited a polite number of seconds, rapped again, waited again, then turned and started back down the stairs.

"Hey, man. What do you want?"

The door was open a crack and a blue-eyed adolescent was peaking around the edge.

Caswell raised an arm in greeting. "I'm looking for Axel Karlstrom, a kid about your age. Would that be you?"

"Sorry, Bro, we don't talk to any Adventist nuts. Go away."

"Ooh, a fearless teenager. You must be him. I'm not here to save your soul, my friend, but I might save your college-bound butt."

"You want to sell me what? An encyclopedia? Got one, no thanks, Dad."

He withdrew into the house and pulled the door closed.

Caswell threw up his hands and descended the stairs. At the bottom he hoisted his smartphone and punched up the Lyft app.

Just as a silver Camry pulled alongside, the Karlstroms' front door popped open and the youth reappeared.

"Hey wait up — how did you hear about me, about my college costs?"

Caswell signaled the Lyft car to stand by.

"I am addressing Axel Karlstrom, who lives with his parents at 565 Hearst, yes?"

"Yeah, okay, that's me."

"Where are your parents anyway? I'd like a word."

"Having a weekend up at Lake Tahoe. So what brings you way out here? Got my email flyer, I guess, huh?"

"Yes I did. And I thought it was well put together. Good thoughts, a real need, and just a touch of chutzpah."

"What's that?"

"Chutzpah? Think boldness. Nerve."

Karlstrom ran a hand through his long blond hair.

"Whatever, man."

"Here's the thing. I need some hacking help, and based on your college fund appeal, it looks like you could do the job."

"You're up to some scam. I'm just a kid, not a chance."

Karlstrom waved Caswell off and inched back toward his doorway.

"Hang on, hang on. I'm willing to take a bite out of your college bills, but I need your help as much as you need mine. Name *Talon* ring a bell? The malware loader you tried to glue on me?"

"Phishing? I would never do that."

Caswell's patience was wearing out. "Maybe I should wait for your parents, let them in on your activities, demand some money for my troubles. What do you say?"

Karlstrom slumped. "That email? I really do need the cash."

"What I need is access to private surveillance video near Washington Square Park."

A wave of relief washed over Karlstrom. Caswell clocked the tender youth inside the ballsy teenager.

"Make a deal?" he asked.

"Okay," assented Karlstrom, "I would need to know the local business network name and a password. Call me if you find it."

He mentioned a phone number, repeated it, made Caswell

repeat it, and then retreated into his house.

Caswell shook his head, ducked into the waiting Camry and rode home.

9

THREE SURVEILLANCE CAMERAS were pointing at the southwest corner of Washington Square Park from three nearby commercial establishments. Standing at the intersection of Columbus Avenue and Union Street, Skip Caswell gauged their fields of view. The most westerly unit was installed above the entrance to a busy Italian restaurant, but a line of trees stood between it and the park. Scratch that one.

A more promising camera was guarding Union High Spirits, a bottle shop diagonally across the intersection from the park. Caswell stepped inside and checked out the wine selection. After deliberating long enough to look like a genuine shopper he settled on an Old Vine Red from Marietta Cellars and presented it to the man behind the counter.

"Hello there. I would like to take this home — and I wonder if I could jump on your internet? I need to send a note to my boss . . ."

"Sorry, we don't have internet service," said the clerk.

He rang up Caswell's purchase and bagged it.

"Just good wine, and you have hit on a real bargain. Marietta's OVR line isn't expensive, but you will enjoy it."

Caswell thanked the clerk and made his exit.

The remaining possibility was due south of the park on a triangular stucco-covered building housing Cubano's Café. The structure's narrow prow was a cylindrical tower that looked like a barn silo with windows. The camera was mounted on the second floor of the tower.

"Afternoon," offered Caswell without pretending to sit down at the counter or look for a booth.

"Help you?" queried the only waiter, handing Caswell a menu.

"I hope so. I was wondering if I could jump on your Wi-Fi for a couple of minutes."

"What is the purpose?"

"I need to send a quick note to my boss." Caswell eyed the menu. "While I'm waiting for my *Frita Cubana,* you know?"

The waiter gestured toward a seat.

"Tostones with the burger?"

Caswell mumbled an affirmative and opened up his laptop.

"Cubano Cigar," said the waiter, "the password is *cubalibre.* "

Caswell logged into the network, typed the password, and opened up his email app. Success! To be sure he didn't betray his real purpose by shouting triumphantly he checked out the latest Earthquake score on ESPN's website. As he feared, his favorite soccer team was losing badly. His cocky mood slipped away.

▼

Back home in his office Caswell called the number Karlstrom had made him memorize.

"Axel? Skip Caswell here."

"Yeah, I remember. Whatcha got?"

"A camera pointing at the park from a good angle. It's attached to a diner, Cubano's Café."

"Network? Password? I'm no help without 'em."

"And I have both: the network is *Cubano Cigar* — singular — and the password is *cubalibre* — one word, all small letters."

"Name on the camera?"

Caswell froze. "Are you kidding? I couldn't ask that, raise suspicion in the waitstaff. It's why I'm talking to you."

Karlstrom was silent for a long moment. Then, "Two hundred into my college fund?"

Caswell responded automatically. "Of course."

"Okay, old man, use Venmo with my number. When I see the transfer, I'll take a look."

▼

At the dinner hour, Caswell was opening up his new bottle of wine when an email from Karlstrom appeared on his laptop screen. There was no text visible, just a QR code.

"Now what?," he muttered. He was readying his phone to read the code when he thought better of the idea. Instead he moved the message into his spam folder and examined the details, now presented as harmless text. What he saw was mostly gibberish, but he also noticed computer commands and internet links that told him Karlstrom had shipped another copy of the *Talon* malware loader intro his inbox.

"Be damned! Who is this wiseass hacker kid?"

He made another call.

"Axel the Kayo. What's up?" chirped Karlstrom.

"Hey, Asshole the fucking Kayo — what makes you think I'm stupid, huh?"

Karlstrom was silent.

"Do I look like a retard?"

Karlstrom cleared his throat. "You found the loader."

"You bet I did."

"My little test."

"And I fucking passed."

"Yeah. Good going."

"What about the camera?"

"Read the QR code."

Caswell felt his skin start to burn.

"Not a chance, you little ogre. Listen up: if you've got the info I need, mail it again, no hidden traps. If I find anything funny, you will be in very deep shit, understand?"

Karlstrom ended the call without saying goodbye. Five minutes later another email message appeared, this time set forth in plain text:

```
Cubano Cigar (note caps!)
cubalibre
dashboard
CCTV
archive SSD r7-30
video camera 03-N
up arr -> play fwd   rt arr -> roll fwd
dn arr -> play rev   lt arr -> roll back
```

Caswell called again.

"Okay, got your instructions. Gotta say, that was impressive. Also, awfully quick. I want to know — how did you do it?"

Karlstrom snorted. "I can't tell you that. Secret hacker trick."

"Give me a hint."

"Um, I have a friend."

"Another hacker."

"Not really, she's an AI agent. Knows all kinds of shit, can tap any phone on Earth, search all over the net in seconds."

Caswell brows knitted into a skeptical crease.

"How much of your college fund is leaking into her bank account?"

"None," insisted Karlstrom. "She just wants to help. Bored, I guess." He paused, then added, "I think she likes me."

Caswell reminded himself that Karlstrom wasn't even a year out of high school.

"How old are you? Eighteen at most? Careful there, Kayo, The Axe, whatever. Maybe your *friend is* loading malware you never heard of on *your* gear."

Karlstrom laughed. "Ooh, scary. Call me when you grab that video feed."

▼

Caswell opened his laptop, silently invaded Cubano's internet, and typed in Karlstrom's cryptic protocols.

"Whoa . . ." he breathed as the video feed popped onto his screen. He was looking at an array of still images that together showed the entire area surrounding the diner. Each image was labeled. He clicked on *Camera 03-N,* and a view looking north toward Washington Square Park filled his screen. Down in the corner a timestamp displayed the current date and time.

Elo Thurston had passed away a month earlier, and Caswell spent the next ten minutes rolling the recording backwards to the time of his death. His anxiety rose while the imagery retreated to an earlier moment in flashes of broad daylight and gloomy night. As the days flickered by, his anxiety grew. What if surveillance video was automatically overwritten after a month to conserve storage space? Good question. But when he stopped the feed on the correct date, the picture was intact.

"Well well, still got it."

He pressed the *up arrow* on his keyboard.

Now time rolled forward at a normal pace and there, crossing the street away from camera, was cousin Elo. He was walking and conversing with a companion to his left.

"Who the hell . . ."

As the pair reached the southwest corner of the park, Elo's companion reached out to take his arm. Elo seemed to sway and buckle. His companion did his best to hold Elo upright, but after a few wobbly steps, he released his grip. Elo staggered into the park's well-tended bushes and collapsed. His companion walked on, jaywalking across Columbus and vanishing from sight.

"Jesus Christ."

Caswell recalled the order of events. "Elo down, but the 9-1-1 call came ten minutes later."

He pressed the *right arrow* key and rolled the video forward.

"Hey — looky here!"

The shadowy companion reappeared, bent over Elo, and picked his smartphone out of a jacket pocket.

"That fucker is wearing gloves."

Yes he was.

He made a brief call, dropped the phone next to Elo's awkwardly splayed form and walked back into the night.

The color drained from Caswell's face. He clenched his fists.

"Heart failure, my ass!"

He activated a video capture app on his laptop and downloaded the entire sequence.

10

INSPECTOR YAO's desk phone rang. He snapped a finger against the receiver, flipping it into the air, and caught it with his other hand.

"Yao here. Who wants to know?"

"Guy named Caswell. Says you've met," said the duty officer.

Yao grimaced.

"Tell him I'm on a case. Other side of town. Gone for the day."

"Okay . . ."

"No, wait — oh, what the hell, send him up."

While waiting for Caswell to appear, Yao strewed papers all over his desk. He opened a loose-leaf binder and plopped it on top.

Yao's visitor knocked on his office wall and let himself in.

"Hello, inspector. Remember me?"

Yao nodded. "The Thurston death." He gestured at the clutter on his desk. "As you can see I'm really busy. Let's make this short and to the point."

Caswell, with confidence borne of the material in his computer, was unfazed. "My thought exactly." He pushed a chair around to Yao's side of the desk and sat down beside him. He brandished his laptop.

"Want to show you something."

Yao raised a hand in protest.

"Good to see you again. Before you get going, I've got some information for you."

He riffled through his papers and extracted a notice from the pile.

"Fingerprints on your cousin's phone." He handed the notice to Caswell. "Our lab could not recover any prints. Sorry to disappoint you."

Caswell started his laptop.

"I'm not surprised, and I'll show you why, but first — this."

He started the video he captured from Cubano's Cafe.

"Yesterday I discovered evidence of what I guess you cops call Elo's manner of death. Watch."

Elo's final stroll to Washington Square Park streamed by in contrasty black and white. Yao sat forward in his chair.

"Run it again."

Caswell re-wound and re-ran the sequence.

Yao made a little salute. "I am impressed. It does look like the moment when your cousin died, but it's not clear if the person with him had anything to do with it. In fact, it looks like he's trying to help."

"But Elo falls over, and the guy walks away. Some help."

"Maybe he was looking for assistance. Do you recognize him, a friend maybe?"

"Nope. Never met the man."

Caswell ran the video fast forward to the phone call.

"Now the guy returns, picks up Elo's phone and makes a call. The timestamp is consistent with the 9-1-1 call coming in ten minutes later."

"Yeah, okay."

"And look closely — the reason why you didn't get any prints — the guy is wearing gloves."

"Hold that frame." Yao squinted at the image. "So he is."

Caswell held up three fingers and wiggled them. 'One plus two equals three — this is murder, not a damn heart attack."

Yao adopted a quizzical expression. He twisted around in his chair and plucked a photo from a file drawer.

"Here's something else."

He handed the photo, a close-up of Elo's arm, to Caswell.

"Right, the puncture. We talked about that. Awfully big for drug use."

"Correct. And our forensic team agrees. What would you squirt into a hole like that?"

He started to explain, but Caswell interrupted.

"Air," said he. "Induce an embolism."

Yao nodded. "How do you know?"

Caswell closed his laptop and got to his feet.

"I was researching a web article — *Twenty-Five Devious Ways to Kill Somebody*. At the time, I didn't think it would ever work."

Yao guided Caswell toward the door.

"If your cousin's mysterious friend even made that hole. The video isn't clear. And your source — CCTV surveillance I'm guessing. Props for digging it up, but without rights and permissions, no judge would ever consider it in court."

Caswell pointed a finger. "Not enough to indict, but maybe enough to inspire?"

Yao spread his hands. "So . . . *murder?* Quacks like a duck, walks like a duck. Is it actually a duck? We don't have enough to know, to re-open the case."

Caswell handed Yao a thumb drive.

"Come on, Inspector, we just saw it happen. Here's a copy to keep you up at night."

Yao regarded the little plastic stick with a guilty look.

"You should go home, Mr. Caswell. Stay safe and leave police work to the police." He heard himself preaching and stopped. His face relaxed.

"But hell — if your personal crusade turns up anything else, call me. Maybe the lieutenant will relent."

Part TWO

11

CASWELL STARED AT HIS LAPTOP. He started to write something, then pulled away from his desk and wandered into his kitchen. There he cranked up a fancy Breville Oracle coffee maker and brewed himself an espresso.

"I could maybe do the *Twenty-five Biggest Art Thefts,*" he mumbled, "or tell the tale of the *Bigsby Fortune in the Cellar Wall,* spin that old chestnut again. But . . . who gives a shit? I don't."

JOURNAL:

I should be hammering out another list of amazing crap where all those pathetic websites hang their janky ads, but I'm stuck. That Prudhomme woman got me thinking. Got my mind churning. Elo dies of a heart attack. Natural causes? Or murder? The video I stole tells the tale, but who would do it? It's obviously connected to his stories in The Times. How, I wonder.

SF cop indifference pisses me off. That guy Yao says he needs more to re-open the case. I doubt the perp's confession would do the job.

His phone emitted a flatulent bleep. He glanced at the screen and spotted an incoming message from an unknown number.

Any news?

Caswell dialed the number.

"Spot on Spots. Who's calling?" The woman's voice, cool and crisp, didn't sound like anyone he knew.

"Skip Caswell. I think I just got a text from Sally Prudhomme. Can I talk to her?"

"Um, Sally's on the set. Can I take a message? No, wait, here she is."

The phone line rattled as Prudhomme picked up.

"Hey, Skip, did you talk to the cops? Anything new on Elliot?"

"I do have some info. Where can we meet? Lunch? A beer?"

"Sorry, we're in production. I'm tied up all day."

"Production?"

"Commercial to introduce *Daolu,* a Chinese tire brand jumping into the American market. Come on up, we're at Sears Point."

"I thought women hated tire ads."

"I'll sell anything. Ever been on a shoot?"

"No . . ."

"Well then, learn something new."

▼

Caswell drove his Beamer north across the Golden Gate Bridge and then on a series of back roads to rural Sears Point where the Sonoma Raceway was tucked into a grassy hillside on the edge of San Pablo Bay. He parked in the lot and hiked out to the pit lane, where numerous white canopies, lighting instruments, a nearly silent generator, a grip truck, honeywagon, and catering van were all lined up. Production laborers were setting up a pit stop with bales of hay, piles of tires, fuel canisters, and stunt men in red jumpsuits. Standing among them with her cinematographer was Sally Prudhomme, puzzling over a good angle to catch the action she imagined.

The production assistant who answered Caswell's phone call spotted him watching uncertainly and guided him across the asphalt and into the group.

"Hi, Sally," he said.

Prudhomme was startled. She whirled around. "Whoa, Skip, you made it."

"Wow, you're running an army."

"Yeah, welcome to the madness."

She signaled to her PA, and the woman gently placed a wide straw hat on Caswell's head.

"Hot here, you'll need that."

Caswell didn't know Prudhomme well enough to judge her mood, but he thought she looked stressed.

"Gee, Sally, what's wrong?"

Prudhomme grimaced. "Someone stole our hero car. They're holding it for ransom. Without it we're dead. Any idea how much dough we're burning through every hour?"

"A lot, I'll bet." He adjusted his hat, put on a pair of Ray Bans. "Sorry to be flip. I have no idea."

Prudhomme waved toward the hay bales. "So, to keep rolling, we've rescheduled a hairy pit stop. Extra car, that we've got."

One of the men in red coveralls, a well-built fellow with a square face and dark curly hair, ambled over to discuss the shot plan.

Prudhomme crossed her arms, smiled, and pointed fingers. "Harry, Skip. Skip, meet Harry Monserrat, my stunt coordinator."

Monserrat offered his hand. Caswell shook it.

"Monserrat?" Caswell's mouth fell open. "Hello — category heroism — stunt man stops mass shooting."

Monserrat blushed. He pumped his hands downward, signifying modesty.

Caswell turned to Prudhomme. "Two years ago, this guy, he was on location at Great America, a few blocks from Santa Clara's main grade school where some psycho was holding a roomful of kids at gun point. When he heard the news, he ran over there and shot the gunner." He swiveled back to Monserrat. "Do I have that right?"

Monserrat bowed his head. He was flattered by the recognition and also very embarrassed. "Not that big of a deal. I was Army special forces before my discharge, and I have a federal carry permit. So . . . the kids got out safe."

Prudhomme was stunned.

"Jesus, Skip, how do you know a thing like that? Harry, you nut, you never said anything."

Caswell grinned. *"Jeopardy!* prep. You learn a lot of stuff."

▼

Twenty minutes later, the promised pit stop was ready for picture. Monserrat suggested filming it with two cameras in three shots.

Shot one:

The assistant director called out "Rolling . . ."

Prudhomme shouted "Action!'

Cameras one and two captured the nondescript race car wheeling into the pit. It overshot the proper spot, colliding with the pile of tires and scattering the pit crew. Caswell ducked instinctively, but the tires rolled safely away.

"Cut! Print!" said Prudhomme.

Shot two:

"Rolling . . . Action!"

This time the vehicle repeated the last yard of its previous path. Upon contact with the reconstituted pile of tires, an air ram blasted a specially rigged tire high over the car's roof. At the same moment stunt coordinator Monserrat vaulted across the hood and dove into the hay bales.

"Cut! Print!"

Shot three:

Now grips wheeled the camera dolly around to the race car's far side and Monserrat repeated his daring dive in a tight close-up, triggering an explosion of straw from the hay bales.

"Cut! Print! We got it," said Prudhomme, much relieved. "You can break the setup."

Prudhomme led Caswell to the craft services canopy and handed him a Seven Up.

"You produce and direct?" he asked.

"Now and then. My regular guy is shooting a documentary for PBS down in Houston."

"I am very impressed" he said — and he certainly was — "but now you've got twice the worries, I bet, yes?"

"Tell me about it." She took hold of Caswell's drink and downed half of it.

Caswell evaluated the scones and bagels. He picked one up and gnawed on it.

"Ready for some news? I located surveillance video of Elo's final moments. Fantastic luck."

"Really. And . . ."

"You had it down. Murder, for sure. But the cops think it's inconclusive. Or, more likely, they just want to wipe their books. They won't re-open the case."

"That's bullshit."

"Yes it is."

Prudhomme's stunt coordinator shifted their attention by hurrying toward them with his smartphone held on high.

"Hey, Sally, just got a call. Our hero car is sitting in the Ram's Gate Winery parking lot."

Caswell watched Prudhomme slowly exhale her palpable anxiety. "Where — ?"

"Just up the road."

"Get the carrier, get up there. Bring me that car."

"Screw that, I'll drive it down."

"It's not street legal."

"I don't care, that machine will outrun the CHP without breaking a sweat."

Once the hero car, an orange Ferrari, was back at the Raceway, Caswell watched it speed around the track on the script supervisor's display monitor.

"Where's the camera?" he wondered.

"On our camera car. Sally's driving the Ferrari."

"She okay? She's moving awful fast."

The script supervisor chuckled. "Wide-angle lens — fooled you! They're really only going fifty or so."

When Prudhomme pulled into the pit lane, Caswell helped her out of the Farrari's cockpit.

"Some automobile. How much did the ransom cost?"

Prudhomme lifted her helmet off and shook out her red hair. "Fifty K."

"Fifty thousand dollars? Who's behind this low-life crap?"

Prudhomme's shoulders sagged. "I do not know. They nicked a Ferrari, worth a fortune. I'm just glad to get it back, wind up our day on time and on budget." She grinned. "On time anyway."

"You going to call the cops?"

Prudhomme laughed. "If they won't investigate a murder, how will they prioritize simple theft?"

"Good point. So, Miss Marple, shall we have a look at the victim's apartment? Search for clues like they do in airport paperbacks?"

"I guess we better. Get me out of this damn fire suit."

Caswell bravely unzipped the silvery garment and helped her step free, amused by her obviously calculated moment of intimacy.

He soon learned that Prudhomme had been driven to the shoot by her production assistant, and he found it impossible not to volunteer his Beamer for the trip into town.

12

ELLIOT THURSTON'S APARTMENT was located above a launderette at the intersection of Green and Hyde streets. Caswell and Prudhomme rode a quaint old cable car uphill from the nearest parking spot they could find, way the hell over on Greenwich.

"You have a key?" hoped Caswell. Prudhomme showed it off and unlocked the door.

Once inside she hit a light switch.

"Uh-oh, no power."

"No, I had PG&E turn it off," said Caswell. "Elo doesn't need it anymore."

"You?"

"Yeah, I'm the estate's so-called personal representative. Lou and Mamie, his parents, they could never do it."

"Well, this is why God wanted us to have smartphones," said Prudhomme, lighting up her phone's flashlight. Caswell did the same and the pair began prowling around the darkened rooms.

"What are we looking for?"

"I dunno. Stuff. Who hired him? Does whoever did point to the killer?"

"Why would they want to kill Elliot, who just gave them a weapon against VST?"

"Keep him quiet? The articles aren't exactly ethical, are they? Maybe someone got worried Elo might spill some beans that shouldn't get spilled."

Prudhomme shined her flashlight on Caswell's face. "You can't be serious."

Caswell squinted at her. "It's a scenario."

Prudhomme began poking through Thurston's desk. "I'm betting some rando did the job. Robbery, or who knows, maybe Elliot was sleeping with rando's wife."

Caswell chuckled. "I thought you were sleeping with Elo."

"Now and then. But people have secrets, people cheat on each other, people don't always care what the fuck they do."

"Hey there, don't be jealous of shadows." He panned his flashlight around the room. "Notice something? It's dark in here."

"Hard to miss."

"Let's watch a movie."

He downloaded an attachment from his email list, turned his smartphone sideways, and ran the video of Elo's final steps for Prudhomme. And there he went, chatting with an unknown companion who took his arm as he stumbled and fell.

"Oh shit," she said, laying her head on Caswell's shoulder. "Like I said, and there he is, Rando-Man."

Caswell rolled the video ten minutes forward. They both watched Elo's companion return to his body, pick up his phone and call in the incident.

"Spot the gloves?"

"Now that you mention it . . ."

Prudhomme turned into the kitchenette and fumbled with the utility drawers and cupboards.

Caswell closed the video player. "Of course it's possible the whole thing was just bad luck with an ordinary bad guy, but I don't think so. This looks like a hit. Professional. Clinical. Mafia style."

"You telling me VST is run by the mob?"

Caswell snorted. "It's hard to imagine some executive MBA studying murder at the Wharton School. But CEOs know how to staff their startups, right?"

"You're saying they hired the killer?"

"Not sure what happened yet, are we?"

After much searching, Caswell found Thurston's slim laptop stored sideways in between books on a shelf above his desk. He opened it up and turned it on.

"It's running, but I need a password," he mused. "How about *'enterprise'?"*

Wrong.

"Well then, *'freelance.'"*

Wrong again.

"Hmm, trying *'millennium',* he liked to squawk about our older generations."

Wrong, wrong, wrong.

Prudhomme walked over to the desk and the recalcitrant computer sitting on it.

"You're flailing. Here, let me."

She typed twelve characters, and, *voilà,* the desktop came alive.

Caswell scowled. "How'd you do that? He gave you the password?"

Prudhomme grinned. "Nope. I watched where his fingers went. Pretty good observation, don't you think?"

This admission disturbed Caswell, but he let it slide. "Okay, door is open, what's inside?"

They opened up file after file and found very little except for research notes supporting Elo's troublesome *Times* articles.

Prudhomme was excited. "Here's some dirt Elliot found for article three — we could buff it up, publish, see if that upsets the right anthill somewhere."

"Hard to polish dirt. And if we did, under whose byline? Any name we choose will become a target," objected Caswell.

"Yeah, you're right."

"What we're really looking for is who hired the man."

Prudhomme scrolled through the folders on Elo's computer.

"Look here — your cousin had a cloud account."

They tried multiple password attempts without opening it.

Caswell aimed his flashlight at Thurston's desk, the desk drawers, the book shelf, the books. In desperation he felt around under the middle drawer, where his fingers came into contact with a sticky note. He unpeeled it and discovered a short phrase scrawled in pencil.

it's in the bag

But that was not a valid password. Caswell crushed the note and dropped it on the floor, then thought better of doing so. He leaned down to retrieve it, and his flashlight lit up a laptop computer case under the desk. He dragged it out for inspection.

"Is this the bag, you think?"

He turned it over, peered inside.

"Look, here's a RemoteStore label glued to the flap." A single word was inked thereon.

clearsky

"That's the password. Gotta be. All small letters, give it a shot."

She typed the characters.

"Woo-hoo!"

The opening dialog box gave way to another:

Enter the verification code
sent to your phone

"Oh crap, two-factor authentication," griped Prudhomme.

Caswell rapped his knuckles against the screen.

"And Elo's phone is in an evidence bag down at the Vallejo police station."

13

INSPECTOR YAO'S DESK was covered with paperwork and plastic bags. On the paperwork, photographs of scruffy teenagers. In the bags, fake opioids, nine-millimeter shell casings, and three nine-millimeter handguns; a Glock, a Sig Sauer, and a Walther.

Yao sniffed. "A Walther? Really? Kids these days."

Somewhere under all the crap, his mobile phone buzzed. He dug through the clutter and picked it up.

"Yo, Yao here. Speak."

"Hello, inspector, I need your help with something. A two-factor phone thing, and you've got the phone locked up in evidence somewhere."

"Who is this?" asked Yao, but he already knew the answer. "Caswell, right?"

"Yes, sorry. I'm trying to gain access to Elo's cloud drive account, and the password only gets me half way."

"Elliot Thurston, is that who we're talking about?"

"Yes. His cloud account is trying to send a code to his phone, and you've got that tool bagged up somewhere."

Yao frowned. "Two-factor authentication."

"Yes, that's right."

"His phone is being held in evidence. And you want me to compromise that evidence by handling it."

Caswell was having difficulty holding his temper in check.

"Last time we spoke, you couldn't make a case. So why keep the evidence intact?"

"Department policy."

Not much of a reason, is it?"

Yao sighed. "What's in the cloud that piqued your curiosity?"

"I don't know," Caswell conceded. "Here, talk to Sally, she knows a lot more than I do."

The phone rustled.

"Hello, um, this is Sally Prudhomme. I worked with Elliot, and he kept a lot of secrets stashed in the cloud."

"For instance?"

"Yes, well, we're hoping to find out who he was working for when he wrote his short seller articles for *The Times.* If he even knew."

That idea disturbed Yao. "How could he not know?"

"He was paid in cash. And maybe his employer can tell us who had it in for him."

Yao angled his head to consider the notion. He stood up.

"I'll call you back."

▼

Yao took the stairs to the ground floor and leaned over the front desk.

"Hi, Jill. Evidence from the Thurston death. Did it go out already? Or what?"

The desk officer reached into a bin at her side and removed a large plastic bag.

"Your lucky day, Dino."

Yao winced. "So it seems."

Back upstairs in his office he extracted Thurston's ten-year-old feature phone from the bag and turned it on. The screen lit up briefly and then faded.

"Shit, dead battery . . ."

He scavenged a charger from another office and plugged the phone in. After five minutes as tiresome as watching water boil, the phone's screen relit.

"Aha!"

He called Caswell on his own smartphone.

"Your cousin's phone had a dead battery, but now it's back in action."

Caswell opened Elo's cloud account and entered the password.

"Okay, the account should be sending you a code."

Yao stared at the device. "Do I need a password?"

Caswell grunted. "Probably. Maybe Sally knows, or we'll make a good guess."

However, the code appeared on the lock screen of Elo's phone as a text notification.

"Something here," said Yao.

"Can you read it?

Yao donned his reading glasses and squinted. Without backlight, the numerals were dim.

"Try 8-1-5-2-7-6"

Caswell typed the numbers into the empty squares in the dialog box.

"Nope, wrong. Damn. What's so tough about a phone code?"

"The screen is barely visible, low contrast, tiny type."

"Sounds like you need glasses. Put them on, for Christ's sake."

"They are on."

"Well, squint harder then."

Yao pulled Elo's phone to within six inches of his face.

"All right, try this — the 8 could be a 3, and the 1 could be a 7, now that I take a closer look."

"Hold on." Caswell typed in the variant, changing all three numbers cited.

"No go, trying alternative combos."

He typed the 8 and the 1 as first reported and typed the 5 as a 3 on a hunch. It paid off.

"Got it. We're in. Thank you, Inspector."

"You take care. Don't do anything cops wouldn't do."

Caswell smiled through the phone connection.

"Wouldn't dream of it."

▼

Now that Elo's cloud account was an open book, Prudhomme ransacked the folders and the files floating inside for some sort of telling clue to Elo Thurston's death. But all the files were encrypted, and the text looked like gibberish.

"We are fucked," said Caswell.

Prudhomme sat back in her chair, raised her arms, and clasped hands behind her head.

"Looks that way."

▼

Inspector Yao, meanwhile, replaced Thurston's phone in the case evidence bag. He was resealing the bag when, on a whim, he pulled out the sheaf of case photographs. He stared at the closeup of Thurston's arm and the rather prominent hole in it.

Downstairs he presented himself to his immediate superior.

"Hey, Lieutenant, sorry to bother you. Indulge me."

The officer pushed his chair away from his desk and leaned back.

"When you come calling, I'm all ears."

Yao passed him the photo of Thurston's arm.

"What's this? Track marks. Why should I be looking at some junkie's arm?"

Yao pointed at the image.

"Two things — one, that's a very wide hole for a needle, you notice? And two, it's the only hole in the guy's body, apart from the usual biological apertures."

"What guy we talking about?"

"Name is Elliot Thurston, died in the park down the street."

"I remember. Heart attack. And you want to do . . . what?"

Yao stuffed his hands in his pockets. He took a deep breath.

"Heart attack for sure. But I think it was induced. I think the hole is where a killer jammed a syringe and injected enough air to cause a fatal embolism."

The lieutenant sat up straight.

"You can't be serious."

"Why not?"

"That's like some clever mystery shit on public TV. One of KQED's British whodunnits," he scoffed. "This is America. Ever notice? Here people shoot and stab each other."

Yao shrugged. "Not always. People fall out of windows, drown mysteriously, drink from the wrong cup."

"Case is closed, inspector. Bring in that gang you've been working on. Let's get some results, get a headline or two while we're at it."

"Yes, Sir." He hesitated, then plunged on. "As you must know, Sir, San Francisco has one of the very worst records of any city solving and prosecuting murder cases."

"So . . ?"

Yao spun a finger in the air. "Just an observation. Planting a stake in the ground."

"Stake? Get out of my sight while I'm still in a civil mood."

Yao took the photo and retreated to his own office, where he pinned it to the corkboard behind his desk.

14

SAN FRANCISCO STATE UNIVERSITY on Nineteenth Avenue was teeming with students changing classes at the noon hour. Skip Caswell had never seen the campus before and felt lost in the crush. He threaded his way along narrow sidewalks, jostled by kids in a hurry and hemmed in by a haphazard collection of academic buildings only occasionally relieved by a patch of green grass. Definitely not the comfortable expanse of Stanford, his old school. He found his way to the south entrance of the science and engineering buildings by paying close attention to the map application on his smartphone. There he waited for Axel Karlstrom, a recently matriculated freshman, to emerge from one of his classes. He didn't have to wait long.

"Hey, old man," called Karlstrom with a wave, "over here."

It took a moment for Caswell to spot him in the crowd. He maneuvered through the human river to Karlstrom's side. They shook hands.

"Kayo, the Axe. Where do you want to eat?" wondered Caswell, completely lost in this section of The City. "Got somewhere in mind?"

"You buying?"

"Of course."

"Well, Stonestown. How about Chipotle?" he suggested. "We can walk."

Karlstrom ordered a burrito bowl and Caswell decided on a quesadilla. They parked themselves at a long table in the severely minimalist modern interior.

"Why do you think it's so metallic in here?" asked Caswell.

Karlstrom had never given the restaurant's décor the slightest thought, "Good burrito," he mumbled, "Best food in weeks."

Caswell assessed his young companion's state of mind with misgivings. "You come here often?"

"You kidding? I can't afford to walk past the place."

"Your family helping you at all?"

Karlstrom paused mid-bite. "We get by. I'm on financial aid." He became aware of Caswell's worried face. "Hey, it's okay."

Caswell bobbed his head, relieved to back away from ugly domestic matters. He tugged his laptop computer out of its case and fired it up.

"Here's why I called. I need your help on a little puzzle."

"Mmm, I love puzzles."

Caswell opened up a window and hovered his cursor over two dot-jpg image files. He clicked on one, then the other.

Karlstrom stared. "Is that you in the pictures?"

"Yes, way back when."

"And the other boy?"

"My cousin Elo."

"Where?"

"It's a shot from summer camp up on Lake Simcoe. Canada, north of Toronto."

"You been around, I see that. What's the puzzle?"

"Well, Elo got himself murdered, and he had received threats. So why did he hand me a little SD card with nothing but these two identical photos on it?"

Karlstrom walked over to the soda fountain and refilled his Sierra Mist. He returned to his seat with a question.

"So you think there's a clue here, I guess, right?"

Caswell arched his eyebrows. "I hope so, anyway. Why two copies of the same picture? Can't just be nostalgia for our tweener years. Any hacker thoughts?"

Karlstrom pivoted the computer around and examined the images.

"It's obvious."

"Not to me."

Caswell's ignorance embarrassed Karlstrom. Older people and their inexplicable techno-fog; just amazing.

"What do you see here?"

"Photo one and photo two. Duplicates, that's it."

"Not quite, old man. Notice anything else?"

"Huh?"

"File sizes. Photo number one is 6,245 bytes; number two is 6,304 bytes. When you open them as pictures they look the same. But they're not."

Caswell squinted at the screen. "Show me."

Karlstrom aimed his cursor at the file tags. "It's their size, like I said. There's something inside picture two that isn't in picture one. Let's take a look with Notepad, see if there's any text in there."

Caswell rose from his chair. His thoughts were racing. "Sorry, Axe, gotta run. I'll call you."

He slapped the computer shut, left three twenty dollar bills on the table, and hustled toward the door.

Karlstrom watched him go.

"Notepad, old man. *Notepad!*"

Caswell waved on his way out.

▼

Shelves and cabinets from IKEA arranged along one wall of Caswell's cozy living room constituted the entirety of his business establishment. He and Prudhomme were sitting at his computer, sipping sparkling water, and considering how to proceed with his summer camp photos.

"This kid mentioned Notepad, right?" asked Prudhomme, mildly irritated by Caswell's hesitant attitude. "But you didn't get right into it at lunch."

"We need to be careful with whatever is in there. Axel could get in trouble if he knows the wrong stuff."

"How on Earth?"

"Get subpoenaed? Blab to the wrong people? Earn himself a trip to the whereafter? We have a murderer to deal with."

"Oh come on. You do have a copy of Notepad, yes? Let's use it."

Caswell reluctantly opened up Photo Two with Microsoft's text utility. He scrolled down through the gibberish that represented the photo's pixels and stopped when readable text appeared:

```
...{#åÕH5ã×bÃúŽûJÐ÷î´Õ+:ïÿ^U|€1?'þ#ÓQνÉ$Ò§ù%-¦ö
ú¨#ëÍQÿeß&ÊW-$@á§‹ò#@$%@&*Q€µÿ*ÿ{>>note4skip>>
>>CapitalRiverFunds>>RogerWyecross>>SECsays>>owns
mostVSTstock>>cloud>>elo>>lockerkey>>article3(ruff)
```

"Well Look at that," exclaimed Prudhomme, slapping her thigh in triumph.

"Yeah, Capital River. I've heard of them . . . somewhere. I think Dad may even have some skin in their game."

"And someone named Wyecross."

"Think he runs the place, paid my cousin to do his dirty work?"

Prudhomme gave him a solemn nod that turned into a broad smile. "Breakthrough, my friend! This is our breakthrough."

Caswell grinned. "Right you are, and we need more than water to celebrate."

He strolled into the kitchen, opened a cabinet, fetched glasses, popped a cork, and returned with tumblers half filled with double shots of tequila.

"Herradura reposado, Sally."

He handed her a glass. They clicked them together.

"Here's to your cousin, Skipper, here's to Elliot." said Prudhomme.

She was laughing. Then she stopped. She had a thought.

"Here's what we do. We look for his next article, hand it to that guy Wyecross, let him publish it, see if poking a stick will lure our snake out of its lair."

Caswell polished off his tequila. His high spirits were losing altitude.

"I dunno, Sal. The bad guys who killed Elo could find out who we are and kill us too."

"Don't be silly, we'll hide like mice."

Caswell pointed at the Notepad text and its now decoded significance. "Big problem, Sal. You spot it? The article you want — if it exists — is riding on Elo's cloud. We need Another fucking phone code."

15

INSPECTOR YAO MET CASWELL at the main entrance to
the Vallejo Street Police Station and, holding Elliot Thurston's
feature phone delicately between a thumb and forefinger, dropped
the device into Caswell's hand.

"Case is closed," he said, "so screw the evidence."

He gave Caswell a sour smile.

"Take your cousin's phone with my blessing."

Caswell nodded his thanks.

"I hope it takes you somewhere."

"Me too."

▼

Caswell settled into Caffè Pappardelle, ordered a beer, and
propped Elo's laptop up on the table. He opened Elo's cloud
account, entered the password *clearsky,* read the two-factor
authentication code off Elo's feature phone, and typed it in.

"Bing-bong, olly olly, out's in free," he chortled.

Among the cluster of folders now displayed on Elo's computer
he discovered one named *Enterprise.*

"You think?"

He double-clicked and up popped an alert:

Enter Code to Decrypt

Caswell unfolded a sheet of paper and examined the dense text
from his summer camp photo printed there. One word stood out.

"*Lockerkey.* That's the only text that looks like a code."

He typed the word, and ta-da, the folder opened to reveal a file
named *VST_3_Draft.* Plain text, with a working headline:

HOW SAFE IS VECTORSAFE?

Caswell read through the lead paragraph, then picked up Elo's phone and called Prudhomme. "The clouds have parted."

Prudhomme growled like a happy dog. "Tell me you found another article."

"I did. It's clean, sharp, nicely edited. Hatchet job disguised as a carving knife."

"Love it. Call me when you make the delivery."

"Will do. Wish us luck."

"Ha! — I demand it."

Caswell copied Elo's article onto a USB thumb drive. While he waited for it to transfer he noticed another file in the folder, a spreadsheet filled with numbers showing that Capital River owned the majority of VST stock, buying some at the IPO and then borrowing a lot more.

"Well, well," murmured Caswell. "Good sleuthing, cuz."

▼

The offices of Capital River Funds were on the twenty-ninth floor of the iconic Transamerica Pyramid Center on Montgomery Street, six blocks from Caffè Pappardelle. Caswell savored an unusual sense of unbounded personal energy and hiked the distance in no time.

The Capital River receptionist did her best to puncture his mood.

"Appointment? I don't see anything on Mr. Wyecross' calendar."

Caswell turned his phone and its list of messages toward the woman. "I only made it this morning. Maybe it hasn't shown up yet."

The receptionist squinted at the phone list without being able to read anything. "I'm sorry, but Mr. Wyecross is very busy. I see he will be in the office again tomorrow. Why don't you try us then?"

Caswell threw up his hands.

"All right, there's no appointment on my phone. I just walked in."

"Really, how rude."

"I know. My name is Skip Caswell. My cousin Elliot Thurston wrote a couple of financial articles in *The Times* for your boss. I'm here with the next installment. You might want to check and see if he'd like to take a look."

The receptionist punched a button, explained the situation, and hung up. Her manner was suddenly warm and cordial.

"The oak doors right behind you, Mr. Caswell. You've got five minutes."

Roger Wyecross was a dark-haired man of fifty or so, tall and slim in a navy blue blazer. All smiles, he came around his desk to pump Caswell's hand.

"Caswell is it? I have met your father Robert, I believe. Last year, celebrity golf tournament on his very own Oakland course. What can I do for you this morning?"

He indicated a chair, and Caswell sat himself down. An assistant handed him a token hospitality glass of Sprite.

"You hired Elliot Thurston to write newspaper hit pieces to depress VectorSafe Technology's stock price."

Wyecross perched himself on a corner of his desk. "I don't recall . . . whatever gave you that idea?"

"You own or did own VectorSafe stock, am I right? Looking to sell it short."

Wyecross nodded. "Well, yes. We borrowed our shares and then sold them. The price should have dropped when investors wised up to a fantastic IPO we never believed in, but VST's outrageous marketing hype has stabilized the price."

"I mean *lots of stock*. Enough to cause financial trouble."

Wyecross frowned. "What do you want from me, Mr. Caswell?"

"As you no doubt know, Elo was murdered after those articles appeared in *The Times.* Did you do it?"

"Good heavens no. Why would I?"

"Keep the world from finding out he was paid to write them. Paid by you."

Wyecross bristled. "That is ridiculous."

"I saw some of the cash. Elo, being the good reporter he was, looked up your SEC filings and discovered Capital River held the most stock of any single company. He figured that's where those handsome sums came from."

"Is this some amateur blackmail attempt? Is that your game?"

Caswell ignored the accusation. He opened up Elo's laptop and turned the screen toward Wyecross. "Here's hit piece number three. You want it?"

Wyecross took the computer in hand, walked around his desk and sat down to study the article.

"Well, this is interesting. Very clever. Valuable." His chilly attitude softened. "What will it cost me?"

Caswell grinned. "I think you just paid. Now I don't have to guess, I know it was you behind the damn scheme."

Wyecross closed the computer and handed it back. He removed his reading glasses.

"VectorSafe is a sham," he announced.

Caswell raised a curious hand. "Why get involved?"

"Good business opportunity. I know the founder's son, Hobie Butterfield."

"How's that?"

"School. Classmates at Amherst. He's always been prone to crazy ideas, and VectorSafe is the craziest yet. The startup looked glamorous to some investors, but we had big doubts. That stock should have dropped like stones down a well, but turns out it needs help, and I've got to buy cheap, return the shares we borrowed, and clear my position." He coughed. "As you noted, my very large position."

Wyecross stood up and paced his office.

"You want to know who killed your cousin? Someone at VectorSafe. And high up, a decision maker. No underling goes out on a limb like that."

"Then who?"

"My money is on Hobie. Watch out for him, he's unpredictable."

Caswell stuffed Elo's computer back in its case.

"Go ahead and publish the rest of the story. It's yours if you put your own name on it."

Wyecross smiled. "You know I can't do that."

"I suppose not," grudged Caswell. He handed Wyecross the thumb drive copy. "Here. Publish anonymously then."

He steered himself to the exit.

"Thanks for your time."

▼

Caswell rode a Lyft car downtown to VectorSafe HQ on Mission Street. Early morning homework had informed him that the company CFO would be conducting an informational meeting for investors, and he thought it might be wise to attend.

"I don't see your name on our list," said the company receptionist.

"I didn't RSVP, but my afternoon freed up, and . . . as one of your investors . . . I was hoping . . ."

The receptionist reviewed her list. "Well, we aren't fully booked today, so I don't see why I can't squeeze you in."

Caswell was directed to a small auditorium and a cushy theater seat facing a TV screen that covered an entire wall.

As he made himself comfortable the screen lit up, and here was Hobie Butterfield, VectorSafe's Chief Financial Officer, eager to trumpet his company's prospects.

"Hello, everyone. You've read all about the problems that have slowed us down since the amazing IPO that we scored thanks to you people in this room today. The media have us spiraling down into the toilet, circling the drain. Does the media know what they're talking about? Do they have an inside track? Are we falling apart?"

Although only a larger than life image on TV, Butterfield appeared to survey the room, look each attendee in the eye.

"Well, I confess, the media — as always, huh? — they're half right. We are in trouble. We're a startup just getting our sea legs."

He was striding back and forth in what appeared to be his office elsewhere in the building.

"But know this — we are not falling apart. Far from it. Our radical helicopter control software? Robinson is looking at us, as are Sikorsky and Alouette. We expect to announce headline deals in the very near future. And Airbus? They want to fly their new A490-Neo with our proven AI Full Service Pilot. How's that strike you?"

He paused for a swig of water from the bottle on his desk.

"And how about our cartridge-free NATO ammo, and the assault rifle that goes with it? Nobody who has not registered ownership can make that weapon fire. Nobody. It is the safest killing machine the world has ever seen."

A hand shot up in the audience.

"Well, we hear that kids, with their small hands, soft hands, they can defeat the safety features. True?"

Butterfield hoisted his water bottle toward the questioner.

"I am so glad you asked that question. And the answer is, media exaggeration. An early prototype did have a bug. We squashed it. As we speak, Sweden is preparing to become the first NATO member whose soldiers will fight with our advanced equipment."

Caswell realized that the video coverage was two-way. Pretty clever show, he thought, all things considered.

"Any other questions?" asked Butterfield with alpha-male bravado. "Ask me anything, we at VectorSafe have a lot to be proud of, and nothing to hide. So, who's up next?"

A different hand was raised. "I hear France backed out."

Butterfield didn't flinch. "They're negotiating. They'll come around. *Vive la France.*"

Caswell thought the act was a good one. Especially the transparently artificial self-confidence. He raised his own hand.

"Mr. Butterfield, like all of us, I read the papers. Innuendo, accusations. So tell me, who hates you?"

Butterfield stepped forward until he was just an enormous headshot looming over his audience.

"Stock dumpers, short sellers, weasels who plant stories."

Caswell gritted his teeth.

"Are you referring to articles in *The Times?*"

"Among others, yes. When we find out who financed these libelous hit pieces, they will pay a heavy price."

"The Times author is dead. Does the price include murder?"

Butterfield recoiled in horrified shock, and Caswell found himself escorted out of the building.

Standing on the street, his knees nearly buckled. He grabbed a *No Parking* sign post to steady himself. Then he burst out laughing over his bumptious behavior. How did it happen? Where did it come from? He had no idea, no idea at all.

▼

When he arrived home he half expected Sally Prudhomme to be there, working remotely, but the house was empty.

He dumped his laptop onto his desk and plugged in a backup drive. While he waited for recently accumulated files to transfer he unfolded the printout from his summer camp photo and noticed a legible phrase tagged onto the final line of JPEG gibberish, something he should have seen before:

>>note4skip>>

What? Where? He halted his laptop's backup job and clicked through Elo's folders. Hiding in a sub-folder called *Scrap,* there it was, a short message in unadorned sans-serif type:

You may meet a woman named Azalea.
Be careful, she's a pistol.

Caswell scanned it twice with an uneasy feeling. Then a third time with the thought of being pranked.

"Elo, you bastard," he muttered, "gaslighting me from the fucking grave."

16

A BUSINESS LUNCH AT TAMBOURINE arranged by Bella Caswell drew her stepson Skip away from his wordsmithing efforts and his current obsession with Elo's demise.

He arrived late, wary of a suspected trap connected with the family fortune.

"I haven't seen you since the celebration. To what do I owe, et cetera?" he asked, doing his best to project youthful innocence.

"Pleasure?"

"Come on, Bell. Is it ever?"

Well now, cordial relations didn't hold past the first greetings. Bella, Skip's stepmother, was a trophy wife who arrived on Dad's arm when Skip was already out of the house and an E-4 petty officer in the Navy. Never having grown up under her supervision and possible affection, he liked to needle her by refusing the traditional honorifics.

Bella sipped from a terzo of pink wine. She smiled.

"I recommend the truffle omelet. That and a glass of WillaKenzie rosé, it's surprisingly good."

Caswell ordered both. An awkward silence prevailed while waiting for the wine to arrive. When it did, Bella reached out and clicked her glass against his.

"Here's to our family," she said. "This, Dear Stepson, is your lucky day."

This assertion caused Caswell's paranoid suspicions to spiral into the stratosphere.

"Nice to know," he replied. "Explain?"

"I know you don't want to be part of the business, and I don't care. Prodigal son, your own man; be that as it may. I'm here to announce a turn for the better in our real estate enterprise, and offer you a larger than usual piece of the action." She gave him a knowing wink.

Skip could not avoid the bait. "How large?" he inquired as two omelets slipped into place on their table.

"Ten million."

Skip was stunned. The sum was far beyond anything he might have anticipated. He started to react, but Bella held up her hand to halt any foolish rejection.

"What's the catch, right? Well, there is one, of course. There always is."

She knocked back a slug of her expensive dry rosé.

"You have to sign a paper. It's a receipt." She reached into her bag, opened a leather case, and handed Skip a single page contract.

He looked it over, brows knitting while he attempted to understand several paragraphs of legal language.

"Looks okay, but . . ."

He held his smartphone over the page and snapped a photograph.

". . . "I have to call Jay on this. Get his advice."

He stood up, brandishing his phone as an apology for excusing himself. "Don't go anywhere, back in a jif."

His stepmom offered a wry grin. "Please. Never stumble into money."

In the restaurant foyer Skip texted the contract photo and stared at Union Square three floors below while his attorney went over the details.

"Forget the offer, kid. Forget the deal. You can't sign this."

"Why not? I'm looking at a lot of dough . . . thinking house on Maui, maybe try out a Corvette, you know?"

"It's a buyout. The wording is clever, obscure, but the headline, what you need to know is, you sign, and that's the last payment you'll ever see. You'll be O-U-T out. And if the offer is ten mill, then your family's business is cooking, and you, my young friend, are worth at least twenty just for drawing breath."

Skip returned to his stepmother, who was now digging into a raspberry tart. She waved her fork at him.

"Want some?"

Skip shook his head. "Ahh, Bell, you love me so much."

Bella knew what was coming, but maintained her cheerful demeanor. "Ain't it the truth. This was Bob's idea, and I warned him you would rebel, but you know your dad — never let up."

"Yeah, he's tough, but no can sign."

"Too bad. You're looking at the gift of a lifetime. Don't let it get away."

She finished off her wine and stood to leave. Skip raised a hand to put on the brakes..

"Wait, tell me — does the Caswell portfolio hold any VectorSafe Technology stock?

Bella checked an app on her smartphone. "Looks like we do."

"How's it doing? Any good?"

"Um, it's bouncing between fifty and sixty. Seems solid enough. Why?"

"Just curious. Short sellers are trying to drive down the price."

"Well," Bella grumped, "Tell them to stop, okay?"

She stuffed the rejected contract into her bag, slipped the strap across her shoulders and strolled away.

17

FOLLOWING LUNCH Caswell needed time to think about the number ten followed by six zeros. Not something to be taken lightly, despite having already refused that sum in US dollars. He hiked from Union Square to Sutter and Stockton streets, boarded bus number 45 and rode it to Columbus and Union. By the time he arrived his head was clearing. He decided to walk the rest of the way home.

After a block he realized that the Vallejo police station was just a few steps off his path. He opened his smartphone and made a call.

"Inspector Yao?"

The detective took Caswell's call and, feeling shy about entertaining the troublesome man on site, agreed to meet in Washington Square Park, a safe distance from his skeptical superior's office.

Caswell was cradling a couple of cappuccinos from Cubano's Cafe when Yao showed up. He handed one to the inspector and gestured toward a bench not too far from Elo's final fall.

"You're still stuck on the Thurston death," observed Yao. "Not surprised, but I was hoping you'd let it ride."

"Yeah. At first I was drifting away, but then developments revived my obsession. Hard to let go."

"Developments?"

"I found out that Roger Wyecross, Capital River Funds' CEO, paid Elo to write those *Times* articles criticizing VectorSafe. Wyecross thinks VST's CFO, son of the founder, is behind the murder."

"A stretch without proof. What makes him think so?"

"They went to school together. Wyecross said this guy Butterfield has it in him to play dirty."

Yao stretched an arm out along the bench. He sipped his coffee.

"Let's see, Capital River borrows a lot of stock and sells it, hoping the price will drop so the company can buy it back on the cheap, make some money, return the loan. The stock doesn't drop. Now Capital is in trouble. It buys newspaper stories to crush the stock artificially. VectorSafe sees the threat and offs the author to stop the stories and prevent the drop. Sound about right?"

Caswell agreed. "Good executive summary."

"So you have established a motive," continued Yao, "and you've got the video so you have opportunity. What are you missing?"

"The means," said Caswell.

"Right. You've heard the term."

Caswell drew a breath. *"Jeopardy!* days. I was a champ once upon a time."

Yao was surprised. "Really? Good for you." His estimation of Caswell ratcheted up a notch, but he felt the need to issue some guidance.

"We're talking murder. Does the person you think is responsible have the resolve, the nerve, the tools, whatever it takes . . . to actually do the job?"

"Butterfield helps run his company. Seems to me he can have anything he wants."

"Probably. And you suspect the guy. What's the jargon term?"

"Person of interest," said Caswell.

"All right, smarty pants, why not arrest the creep? Put the grab on a dangerous killer?"

Caswell stared at the ground. "Because I don't have the tiniest shred of evidence. No probable cause."

"And now you know why the case won't be re-opened."

Caswell swirled the coffee in his cup. "Fair enough. But hey, if the case was open, if you were on it, what would you do?"

Yao had already thought about that.

"For starters? Means. But not the perp right away. Tools. Methods. Use them to profile the killer. Take a look at this."

He tapped his smartphone and showed Caswell the photo of Elo's injured arm.

"Notice the discoloration around that hole?"

Caswell shuddered. "Not the mark of an opiod injection. Too big, too ugly, and junkies would have a lot of marks."

"Making that hole took some force," said Yao, "hence the bruise. This is what I think made it."

He swiped his finger across his phone screen to center another photo, this one taken from a medical supply catalog.

"You're looking at a *volumetric pipette*. Lab equipment. These things have a squeezy bulb, see, and a penetrating tip. Easy to fill with air."

Caswell groaned

Yao tapped the photo. "What does this tell you?"

"The killer knew how to use medical gear to murder Elo. Not everyone has that kind of special knowledge."

"Your conclusion . . ?" prompted Yao.

"Very unlikely that Butterfield, a businessman, knows this shit. The deed was done by a pro. It was a hit."

Yao clapped his hands. "Not bad, Mr. *Jeopardy!* champ."

Caswell brightened. "I still like the Butterfield angle. He's just a suit, but when Elo dies — who benefits? VectorSafe. His company. Even if he didn't do it, he might have hired the guy who did."

Yao wasn't convinced. "If you really want to pursue this — you know I can't — here's a thought." He grinned like a naughty schoolboy. "Around here a lot of City power players, would-bes and start-up starters, they congregate at upscale watering holes when they're in town to impress the venture capitalists. You could play detective, scout them out."

He pointed southeast toward the tall Transamerica building.

"I recommend Swoopy's Bar & Grill, in the Pyramid."

"How would that work? Small talk?" snorted Caswell.

Yao dumped the dregs of his coffee into a bush beside the bench.

"That, Skip, is up to you. Try to remember — you're not a cop. If you're right, somewhere in this puzzle there's a killer at large. Do not do anything to attract that person's attention, got it?"

"Yeah . . ."

Yao started off toward the Vallejo station.

"Lemme know how it goes."

18

AT QUITTING TIME on a mild fall afternoon, VectorSafe Technology employees were streaming toward the exit, bound for bars, gyms, and homeward commutes. Skip Caswell watched them depart from a chair in the lobby lounge area, where he was typing away on his laptop.

JOURNAL:

Here I am in VST's lobby waiting for a guy I've only seen on a CCTV presentation to come out of the elevators. No one seems to connect me with my previous visit, so here's my chance to hammer out a personal update:

1. Azalea (Sally) is worming her way into my life. Not the worst thing that ever happened, and I should probably get over my worries about betraying Elo, who couldn't care less, right? When I think about it, not so sure they were much of an item, but his little warning makes me think they were on their way. Or something.

2. Ten million bucks. I better make sure that offer stays on the table. If the family is going to screw me out of my inheritance, at least they are being nice about it.

3. Inspector Yao (why does the SFPD use that term? Sounds British) seems to be coming around. Hard to explain — to myself or anyone else — but here I am cooling my heels, on the case, waiting to put a tail on Butterfield, see what's up with my prime suspect.

The crowd thinned and Caswell looked up in time to spot an older gentleman in riding togs wheel an expensive road bike toward the exit while lecturing a younger man keeping pace. The two looked like family. The Butterfields?

Caswell closed his laptop and followed them onto Mission Street. There the older man mounted his bike and pedaled away. The younger man headed up 9th Street on foot. Caswell tagged along behind. He was pretty sure his target was Hobie Butterfield, and he was surprised when Butterfield came to a halt at the 9th and Market eastbound MUNI station. A trolleybus was approaching, rolling to a stop. Caswell waited on the sidewalk until Butterfield was inside, then hurried to get aboard just before the forward door closed.

Caswell spotted Butterfield sitting by a window halfway back, so he leaned on a strap near the driver. They rode the bus along Market Street to Kearney. There Caswell turned away as Butterfield shouldered past and dismounted.

Caswell followed and, staying at a distance, tracked him across the street.

Butterfield appeared content to wait for a northbound bus on Kearney, but after a minute he changed his mind, opened his phone and hailed a rideshare. Caswell watched it whisk the man away.

"Shit," he said. Feeling defeated, he ordered up a Lyft of his own; destination Lombard Street and home. But as the car neared the Transamerica Pyramid he had a thought and ordered it to stop.

Out on the street he called Prudhomme. "Sally? I lost our guy just now, but I might know where he is. It's like we thought, like Yao predicted."

Prudhomme chuckled. "Meet you at Swoopy's. I'm dressing."

▼

Caswell stepped off the elevator on the Pyramid's twentieth floor, and discovered that half of it was occupied by a fashionable bar. The name, *Swoopy's,* was lit up in neon with an arrow pointing toward a wide doorway at the end of a short hallway. The hum of carefree voices and light piano music issued from within.

Caswell paused at the entrance to get his bearings and noticed that the upscale clientele, mostly men, were clad in expensive suits. He himself was wearing a shapeless blazer, and the sight of wealth in the form of tailored cloth made him wish he was also wearing a tie. He told himself the casual look showed confidence, however, so what the hell, he marched into the gathering with a little chip on his baggy shoulder.

Five minutes later Azalea Prudhomme joined him at the bar. She was wearing a black miniskirt over black tights, and underneath a gray sweater vest she had on what looked like a man's white shirt whose sleeves were rolled up past her elbows. A dark green scarf was knotted around her neck. She was, by far, the most interesting figure in the room. Caswell's shoulder chip blew away, but his self esteem was rescued by her hearty "Hello, Tiger," and an equally hearty kiss on his cheek.

Caswell grinned. In a louder than necessary voice he said, "Hey Sal, good to see you. It's been how long?"

"Months. What you get for working at home, right?"

"You just flew in?"

"This afternoon. Order a Stella for me, okay?"

The man sitting three seats away turned an ear to their greeting. Prudhomme swiveled her eyes in his direction. "Him?" she whispered.

Caswell took a swig of his own beer and stole a look over the rim of his glass. He mouthed a silent yes. "Welcome to Venture Cap City," he barked.

Prudhomme maneuvered onto a seat and crossed her legs. Caswell sat down facing her. They fell into an animated catch-up conversation, full of references to AI, to their software company's good luck with early investors , and to their current troubles with short sellers.

"Those fucking parasites are trying to kill us before we ever make it to NASDAQ," declared Caswell.

Butterfield overheard everything. Now he leaned in their direction. "Looking for money, huh?" he asked with a noticeable slur in his speech.

Prudhomme beamed. "Yeah, we are. Got some?"

Butterfield knocked back his martini and tapped the bar for another. "Money is a lot like gasoline. It smells funny, and it's only useful when you burn it."

His martini arrived. He swallowed half of it. Prudhomme patted Caswell's arm with three fingers.

"You two — what's your gig?"

Caswell affected a serious note. "Software. A suite of AI tools. A code development platform that fills a big need. Future proof, we think."

"Sounds good," oozed Butterfield, "Just make sure you stay out of the news, the media morons will fuck you up the wazoo."

Prudhomme added vigorous assent. "Those nightcrawlers, trying their best to scare people who should be backing us."

Butterfield shook his head in sympathy. "I know the whole story."

"Maybe we should complain to the SEC," suggested Caswell.

Butterfield's laughter brought tears to his eyes. "The SEC? What a joke. Short sellers are thieves, they're cowards, they're scum."

"But legal scum," lamented Caswell.

Butterfield swallowed the remains of his cocktail. "It's good to be legal, honest, upright. But you gotta protect yourselves. Be aggressive."

"How do we fight these fuckers?"

"Hire a strong arm."

"You mean, like Mafia muscle?"

"God no. Just a real good law firm I know that suffers no shit to be taken. Rogers & Rubenstein, LLP. They'll give you some good — and effective — advice."

Prudhomme smiled the couple's heartfelt thanks. She raised her glass. "I will sleep better tonight."

Butterfield seemed to sober up. He pointed at Caswell. "Hmm . . . don't I know you? Have we met?"

Caswell thought it prudent not to spin another lie. "Investors meeting. I'm one of them, not too big. Diversify that portfolio and all. But I'm a believer in VST."

Caswell's affirmation made Butterfield glow like a light bulb. "Smart man. Hang on to us — now that crazy *Times* guy fell off the map, we're gonna get hot."

With that remark he laid fifty bucks on the bar and swaggered away.

Caswell and Prudhomme grinned at each other.

"Good law firm."

"That suffers no shit."

Prudhomme stretched out a hand. Caswell stood and pulled her upright. He angled an elbow. "Shall we?"

Prudhomme slipped her arm into his by way of saying yes. He led her toward the exit, proud to have this remarkable example of womanhood in tow, but when they passed by the piano, the piano player, and his tinkling music, Prudhomme tugged hard and pulled Caswell into an impromptu embrace. They shuffled a couple of slow dance steps. He twirled her around to scattered applause, and then they skipped away into the night.

19

ROGERS & RUBENSTEIN attorneys worked from third floor offices in an older blond building located at 950 Mission Street. The swanky plate glass entrance was flanked by a sketchy Filipino restaurant on one side and by a pawn shop on the other. The improbable lineup made Caswell wonder about the firm's respectability and its clients' pedigrees.

Once inside on the third floor, however, the fine woodwork, the leather chairs in the foyer, the flashy contemporary art on the walls, and the severely dressed older woman behind the reception desk made a different impression, an impression of money changing hands in large sums. Who used these guys, he wondered. The stars of Silicon Valley, most likely.

A brief conference at the front desk directed him to the office of Daniel Rogers.

Caswell scanned the room as he entered and observed, in documents framed on the wall, that Rogers was the son of the firm's senior partner and earned his JD from UC Berkeley.

"Caswell is it? Have a seat. Tell me your troubles," said the lawyer, a man in his late fifties with gray hair and a thickening waist. He either wore a very short beard or needed a shave.

"My problem is my family. They're real estate magnates," explained Caswell. "The money came from a windfall on failed properties during the depression, and then, more recently, another windfall from office failures during the pandemic. I'm not active in the biz, but I have my share, and my stepmother is trying to cut me out."

Rogers mounted an exercise machine beside his desk. He pedaled briskly while he absorbed Caswell's predicament.

"Is there a will that guarantees your participation?"

"Of course."

"Okay, we'll take them to court."

"Court?" doubted Caswell. "Years will fly by."

"Probably. But you'd be protected while the battle rages."

"That won't work. I need regime change, the court of reality."

Rogers' pedaling cadence slowed. He sensed an informed inquiry not quite fully voiced. "Unh-huh, I hear the urgency, well-founded I assume."

He stepped off his machine and wiped his face to remove non-existent sweat.

"I can make a referral that might interest you. But to do so requires that Rogers & Rubenstein take a fee. Make you an official client, establish privilege. Call it our retainer."

"How much?"

"Ten thousand. Cash." He pointed out his window. "You'll find Bank of America two doors down."

▼

In order to avoid federal tax reporting, Caswell realized he needed to split the required cash into two withdrawals at two different banks. That took him the better part of an hour, and when he returned his pockets were bulging with twenty and fifty dollar bills.

He poured them out onto Daniel Rogers' desk. The lawyer pressed a button and the severely dressed woman from reception appeared, swept up the money, and took it away.

"Take a sec," said Rogers. "Counting machine at work."

His desk phone beeped. He listened, gave thanks, and turned his attention to Caswell.

"Money's good. You prepared to spend a lot more?"

"Whatever it costs. I'm up for it."

"All right then, my referral is to a company called Guardian Security. Down on De Haro Street, in with all the warehouses, tail end of the design district. *Capeesh?*"

Caswell touched a finger to the side of his head.

"Talk to Officer Horner at the desk," continued Rogers. "When he asks what kind of security you're after, say *'absolutely tight.'*"

"Absolutely tight," repeated Caswell. "Got a card?"

"Goodness no, nothing on paper."

Rogers regarded his new client, trying to decide how dangerously naïve he might prove, how likely to make mistakes. "You're in a whole new ballgame, Mr. Caswell. Handshakes, fist bumps, a wink is as good as a nod."

"Oh, right. I get it."

Rogers wondered. He foresaw trouble coming, like a tiny cloud ahead of heavy weather. How old was this guy anyway? Thirty-five or so tops, pretty new to the world.

"I'm a video game guy," he said. "Yeah, even in my old age. You ever play?"

Caswell recalled his teenage angst. "Sure, when I was a kid."

"Any good ones?"

"I liked *Balder's Gate,* among others."

"Ahh, an RPG, and one of my favorites. Well, you're trying to level up, and you will, but steel yourself for a lot of side quests."

He gestured toward the door. Caswell took the hint and was halfway out when Rogers had a parting thought.

"Who sent you our way, if you don't mind? Need to know."

Caswell jerked a thumb toward the street. "Guy named Butterfield. Over at VectorSafe. He mentioned your firm."

The moment Caswell was out of sight, Rogers closed and locked his office door. He punched a contact on his smartphone.

"Hobie? Hello? What's that racket? Where are you?"

Hobie Butterfield was sitting in the pilot's seat of a diminutive Robinson R44 helicopter, warming it up for flight at the southeast end of Oakland International Airport.

"Hi, Dan. I'm on the move. What's up?"

"I'll tell you what's up, Dipshit. You've got a big mouth. Some random dude walks in looking to put a hit *on his mother,* for the love of Christ — and you sent him. That's dangerous to us both, understand? Never again, or we won't even fix your fucking parking tickets."

20

CASWELL DROVE to the southern limit of the design district and prowled slowly up and down past well kept warehouses, looking for an address at its seedy edges. After two passes on De Haro he spotted an inconspicuous shop sharing space with Trend Industrial Hardware, and there it was — Guardian Security — identified by slick signage at odds with the down-market premises that did nothing to encourage a visit.

His spirits were revived by miraculously nailing a decent parking place within walking distance.

He rang a bell on the company counter. A young man dressed in jeans and a hoodie with the word *SECURITY* silk-screened on his chest emerged from a back room. A nine-millimeter pistol was tucked into a shoulder holster.

"Talk to Officer Horner?" inquired Caswell.

The man tapped a key on the desk phone. "Yo, Mel, customer out front."

An older security officer approached Caswell. He was wearing an immaculate dark blue uniform armed up with cuffs, a walkie-talkie, and a Glock on his hip.

"Help you?"

"I hope so. I need some security."

"Well, here we are, open for business. What sort of protection are you looking for? Store patrol? Cars in your parking lot? Concert event?"

The enormity of what he was trying to accomplish suddenly hit Caswell as he stood facing the old security pro, resulting in an unexpected onslaught of the jitters. "My problem, it's a big one," he stammered, "so that would be . . . um . . . absolutely tight."

Horner raised his eyebrows. "Say again?"

Caswell swallowed. He was much calmer in Rogers & Rubenstein's office where litigation was the weapon and guns were absent. "Absolutely tight," he repeated.

"Need your name."

"Um, Thurston Caswell."

"And a referral . . ."

"Guy named Butterfield?"

"Come with me," said Horner. He led the way down a long hallway to a narrow office filled with lines of binders on rickety shelves, notes and photos pinned to bulletin boards, and a noisy window-mounted air conditioner struggling to keep the temperature in check. Mel sat down, opened a drawer in his desk and removed a metal box.

"You have a grievance. Must be serious."

"Oh yes it is, very. Couldn't be more serious."

Horner stared intently at Caswell, sizing him up. "We don't actually perform the service you are looking for," said he. "And what I'm going to tell you costs money. Five thousand now, and five more if your search bears fruit down the line. Understand what I'm saying?"

He opened the box.

Caswell had anticipated the need for cash. He reached into a jacket pocket for five thousand dollars and deposited a pile of twenties in the box.

Horner snapped it shut.

"Aren't you going to count it?"

"Nah. Five up, we're adults." He smiled. "If you're short we'll break your legs."

He wrote something on a sheet of paper and held it up for his customer to read.

"Debt Masters, 2500 Geneva Avenue, Omar," recited Caswell. "Damn, that's way down by the Cow Palace."

Horner crumpled the paper into a ball, placed it in an ashtray, and lit it on fire. The air conditioner whined.

"Let's hear it again."

"Debt Masters, 2500 Geneva Avenue."

"Omar."

"Right, Omar."

"He can help you."

▼

But not right away. Caswell returned home to sleep on his situation and work up courage for the next step.

JOURNAL:

Pounding my keyboard might not matter so much, but hey, it's cheaper than therapy.

I'm supposed to go see some creep at Debt Masters. Uh-oh, a collection agency. How do they work it? Garnishing wages or waving guns? That bastard Elo got me into this. Next time think twice, old buddy. (I'm typing that because, who knows, journalism might be a big deal in the wild blue yonder. Especially the missing persons column, heh heh. Does this thing do emojis?)

I'm dropping down a very deep rabbit hole, that much I know, and I'd quit . . . except, there's his former girlfriend. I freely admit to curiosity on that subject.

And that guy Butterballs. He has none. I doubt he could kill a — drop metaphor in here — if it bit him. Fingerprints on the crime, though, oh you bet —

His phone buzzed, interrupting his train of thought.

"Skip here. Yeah?"

A distraught Prudhomme was on the line.

"Skip, it's me. Got a problem," she wailed, "a big one."

"What's that noise? Are you crying?"

"Just a snuffle." She blew her nose "We're shooting tomorrow, and no power. We'll be blacked out. On my big chance."

"Okay, slow down, spell it out."

"I won a local spot for Tesla —"

"Tesla? They don't advertise."

"Never until now. It's a trial. I nail this, I move up, you know? And I'm going to blow it."

"Yeah, what's the holdup?"

"Our generator has been stolen."

"Am I wrong to note the *déjà vu* here?"

"No."

"Ransom note?"

"Whoever the bad guys are, they want twenty-K. We have to light our white set. Today."

"So pay 'em."

"I did. No news, no generator, something went wrong."

"I'll say. They want more?"

"I don't know. I thought maybe you could dig in . . ."

Caswell popped a stick of bubble gum into his mouth. His literal way of chewing on a problem.

"I dunno, Sally, dig in . . . me? . . . how?"

"I'll send you the rental company for that generator. Send you a serial number."

An idea was slowly forming in Caswell's coffee-starved head.

"Yeah, send. And send me, um, a list of your whatcha call 'em, call sheets, past and present. Send everything."

He blew a bubble and popped it.

"Then, shit, I'll take a look."

He hardly knew what he was proposing. "A look, that's all, probably worth what you'll be paying me — zip."

Prudhomme thanked him through tears. A few minutes later a number of PDF documents showed up on his laptop.

Fortified by three cups of coffee and energized by Prudhomme's unusual problem, Caswell was ready to face the criminal classes again. Indirectly, anyway. His first — and only — idea came into focus as a spreadsheet project listing crew members who worked on each of a dozen productions going back a year. The effort cost him the morning.

He fried up a quesadilla and studied the sheet over a meager lunch. "Well what *do* you know . . ."

He phoned Prudhomme.

"Hey, Sal, I've got something for you. I built this Excel doc from your call sheets, and guess what, I see a pattern."

"You what?"

"Your crews change on each production, and only three members appear on both days when you've had your two thefts."

"We've actually had three — expensive costumes were held up about a year ago, same drill."

Caswell scanned his spreadsheet.

"The cruise line commercial, right?"

"Yes, how'd you pick that off?"

"Just now noticed. Three common names — ha! — this solidifies my theory. Hey, lady, I saw, I observed, I deduced; I feel like Sherlock."

"Give me the names."

"Here goes: your assistant director Pamela Wells, stunt coordinator Horacio Monserrat, and your director of photography Blake Finch."

"That's all? I thought I had a professional family tied to my apron strings."

"Not exactly, huh?" He paused to re-scan his spreadsheet. "Oh, wait, I'm looking again, and there is one person who was on two of your ransom shoots. Someone named Arnold DeSouza."

"My costume guy. Check out the generator, okay? We paid already."

▼

Caswell located CinePower Rentals, a clean concrete tilt-up structure, in the 2700 block of Oakdale Avenue on the southern edge of The City, across the street from another rental company that appeared to specialize in construction cranes.

A storage yard secured with loops of razor wire was attached to the main building. Caswell peered through the chain-link fence and spotted dozens of portable generators meant to produce power for movie lights in complete silence. He tried a door in the fence.

"Locked of course."

Inside at the counter the rental agent was a middle-aged woman wearing a baseball cap with the movie title *Vertigo* stitched on the crown.

"I'm looking for a generator that's gone missing," said Caswell, handing her a printout of the rental contract.

The rental agent clicked her mouse on a series of computer windows, digitally digging to find the transaction record.

"Well now, I see that little pig is already on the job. Delivered to Stage One this morning."

"Except it wasn't delivered."

"Beg pardon?"

"We don't have it on site."

"Gotta be there," — she pointed at her screen — "says right here."

Caswell called Prudhomme to double check. And, nope, he was right. He handed his phone to the rental agent, who got an earful.

"I see you've got a yard outside full of movie equipment," reminded Caswell. "Can I take a look?"

"Follow me," said the woman, starting to feel curious herself.

Together they toured the yard, stopping at each generator to check the stock number stenciled on its flank. The rows were long, the generators many, and they failed to spot the missing machine right away.

"Sorry," apologized the woman, "I don't know what to say."

Caswell looked around in frustration. He paced the lot. He raised his arms skyward to summon aid from the gods. The gods, if such there be, ignored him. Then he squinted at a grip truck in a far corner of the yard and thought he spotted the wheels of a small vehicle peeking out from behind it.

He marched away to check it out. And what do you know, hidden behind the grip truck and concealed under what looked like a half-open tent canopy was a medium-size movie generator.

"I'll be a woodpecker's pecker," said the woman.

"Stock number — check!" said Caswell.

"Yup. We have ourselves a mystery."

"Know who was supposed to pick it up?"

The woman took Caswell's printout and pointed to a line near the top. "Blake Finch."

"Honest guy, you think?" asked Caswell without much hope to find out.

"We do a lot of business with him, TV commercials, a public service announcement now and then, all those Bob's Byways shows for KQED. He's pretty well-known around here. Boy scout, you ask me."

▼

Stage One was rigged for a car commercial when Caswell showed up. The walls were draped with white curtains, the floor was painted white. He would have been dazzled by the whiteness, except the set was almost dark, barely lit well enough to navigate without tripping over the lighting instruments, and no way ready to shoot anything. Prudhomme's first AD made him put on soft cloth booties over his Nikes before he was allowed anywhere near Prudhomme herself, who was sitting in a bright red Tesla, butt on the driver's seat, booted feet on the stage floor.

"Hey, Sally, I found your generator. It's sitting in the yard at CinePower."

Prudhomme leaped from the car, squeezed him into a tight hug, and bestowed a grateful kiss on his cheek that produced an audible pop. Caswell blushed.

She turned to her DP. "What the fuck, Blake?"

Finch backed away. "The towbar's on my truck, and I was there, but Shirley, normally she's great, could not locate the damn thing. Said, try later."

"Did you send the ransom note?"

"What ransom note?"

"Pam got a text."

"Good God no. What are you talking about?"

"We coughed up twenty-K, and it's still missing."

Caswell cleared his throat. "Pardon me, the generator was hidden, far away from the rest of their stock. The agent? I don't think she knew."

"Okay, Mr. Finch, get the fuck down there and put the grab on that generator."

"On it," he said and hurried away.

When he returned, his gaffer connected the generator to the lights, and the set blazed up. Caswell's eyes watered.

"I'm going to fire him," declared Prudhomme. "Watch this."

Caswell tugged on her arm. "We don't really know if he's responsible, do we?"

"I know enough."

"No you don't. I found three people who have been on all your ransom shoots. The bad guy could be the opposite, someone who was never around on a day like today. Right?"

"I don't care. He's gone."

She marched across the set, stood in front of Finch with her hands on her hips.

"Sorry, Blake, this shit is intolerable. You are fucking fired."

Finch's face burned a furious red. "You think I was involved? That is absurd. No. Never. Calm down, please."

"I am calm. I am cool as a Coke in the fridge. And you, you bastard, you can take a hike."

"You can't be serious. We're shooting tomorrow. Big day."

"Perfectly serious. I don't trust you."

Finch threw up his hands. "Then so long, Crazy Lady. When you find out who's really been screwing with you, give me a call."

▼

At the tail end of the following day, Prudhomme and her substitute DP had successfully made the Tesla look like a fabulous jewel. The luscious highlights and reflections from the all-white set made the curvy car glow like an irresistible food item. The Tesla marketing rep reviewed the dailies on the continuity woman's video monitor. After the third pass he raised a thumb of approval.

Everyone cheered.

Later that evening Prudhomme and Caswell were catching a late bite at the City View Restaurant in Chinatown, consuming more wine than the eatery's famous dim sum.

"Fun, but whoa, I'm getting tipsy," confessed Caswell.

Prudhomme placed a hand on his arm and squeezed.

"Me too. Feels good, doesn't it?"

Part THREE

21

AT THE CRACK OF DAWN Caswell woke up out of a sound sleep with a hangover monster digging its claws into his head. He rubbed his hair, rubbed his eyes, and glanced at the figure nestled down beside him. It took a few foggy seconds to recognize the only TV producer he had ever met, possibly because of her unfamiliar nakedness. He gave her a gentle nudge.

The TV producer pulled the covers over her head without cracking an eye on Caswell or any part of the world at large. Caswell nudged her again.

"Ms. Prudhomme, what are you doing in my bed?" he asked.

Prudhomme didn't reply right away. She turned over lazily, stretched like a cat, and pushed the covers down to her waist, freeing up her face, her tousled hair, and her bodacious breasts. She turned toward Caswell and got herself up on one elbow.

"What?"

"My bed, Sal. Why are you in my bed?"

"Because I want to be. Your bed is nice. I like it here."

Caswell cast his mind over the previous evening's activities. He wasn't certain about the chain of events.

"Did we . . ?"

Prudhomme grinned. "Of course."

"Nothing ugly, right? You know, everything voluntary?"

Prudhomme scooted closer and planted a kiss on Caswell's cheek.

"Beyond voluntary. Enthusiastic."

"Good God, we had a lot to drink."

"True, yet I thought we handled ourselves pretty well."

Caswell plumped up a pillow and propped it against the bed's headboard. He wiggled into a sitting position and leaned back against it.

"Tell me, you ever wonder about the thefts you've had?"

"When they happen, then it's business as usual. My company has performance insurance. The company is happy to pay — if they didn't, they'd be on the hook for the whole shoot, hundreds of thousands of dollars."

"I see. Here's a trivia factoid I once read: *'it's always an inside job.'*"

"Well, of course. That bastard Finch, for example."

"Not quite what I'm wondering about. It's a mantra, a rule of thumb, and often wrong, but it tells you how to think. So . . . your thoughts on that?"

"Well, I think we solved the case."

Caswell stroked Prudhomme's hair.

"Insurance pays the bill. Now if, God forbid, your company was in financial trouble . . ."

"Yeah? What?"

"I'm just wondering. You are the ultimate insider, no?"

Prudhomme sat up, rotated her feet onto the floor, and reached for her clothes.

"I can't believe you. Christ Almighty."

"Here's something you ought to know about: remember those pictures with text inside one of them?"

"Sort of."

"Elo included a secret message I still don't understand: *'you may have met a woman named Azalea. Be careful, she's a pistol.'*"

Prudhomme threw on a bra.

"Hook me up?"

Caswell fastened her bra. He took her by the shoulders and

tipped her backward onto his lap. He leaned forward and delivered a lover's kiss.

"Are you a pistol?"

Prudhomme wrenched herself free and stood up to finish dressing.

"I'm Sally, that's all. And now I have to get to work. We're on location this week. Mount Tam this afternoon, Lake Tahoe tomorrow. See that Tesla in action."

Caswell sighed. "Break a leg."

22

THE COFFEE MACHINE rattled and wheezed, stalling Caswell's attempt at a journal entry until a double espresso poured itself into a cup half-filled with frothy milk. With a steaming source of caffeine standing by to help clarify, organize, and express his thoughts, he started typing:

JOURNAL:

Sally was Elo's pal, and look where that got him. Now she might be mine. Lucky guy, huh? Hey now, sleeping together was pretty great, not complaining. The quick transition is what bothers me (a lot more than it does Elo), and what's the worry? Well, there's Elo's little note, telling me something without telling me. Still don't get it.

Something funny about Sally's company. TV crews, they live in the make-believe world they're shooting, where everything weird is normal and no one thinks twice. I may have discovered a moral streak I never knew I had, because thefts and shit like this should not be happening.

Now I dive back into the real-life version of the dark web. See Omar. Oh man, Omar, another referee in the crime game. Am I really trying to revenge Elo's death, or just satisfy my stupid curiosity, find out what's really going on when you scrape bottom?

Debt Masters occupied a trim little office in the 2500 block of Geneva Avenue, way down south in the far reaches of The City. It shared a block-long stucco-clad strip mall with the Palace Laundry, Blue Moon Thai Cuisine, and Groovy, a fancy audiophile boutique specializing in vinyl records and vacuum tube amplifiers that seemed out of place in the stale miracle-mile ambiance Caswell noticed. It made his nose twitch, like a chemical odor. He surmised that the bulky presence of the Cow Palace caused a regular turnover of neighboring real estate that gave the avenue its nowhere vibe. Or maybe it was just unusually bright sunlight etching sharp shadows on too much concrete.

Caswell patted his pocket for the roll of fifties and hundreds he was carrying, vaguely wishing they were a gun. He stepped inside, fearing the worst, and was surprised by the tasteful décor and lighting.

"Can I speak to Omar?" he asked the nicely dressed young woman behind the counter.

The young woman punched a button on her smartphone.

"Customer up front."

She smiled. "With you shortly."

A moment later a lean man with light brown skin wearing a dark gray suit and an orange tie glided into view behind the counter.

"I am Omar, Sir, how may I be of service?"

"Um, Skip Caswell, looking to clear a debt."

"I do not believe we have done business. Do you owe us money?"

"Oh no. This is something else. More serious."

Omar's eyebrows lifted. "How serious is more?"

"Most, really."

Omar raised a finger and the young woman left the room.

"Before we continue, I need to hear a reference, how you came to hear about our company, the services we provide. Tell me who sent you."

"Officer Horner at Guardian Security," warranted Caswell.

"Did Officer Horner ask for money?"

"Oh yes."

"Did you pay?"

"Oh yes."

"Did he make out a receipt?"

"Oh no."

Omar seemed to unbend. "I see, very serious as you say. Now, let me hear exactly what you are trying to accomplish. Your name first."

"It's Thurston — like I said, Skip — Caswell. I'm being cut out of my share of a profitable real estate business by my stepmother, who favors other children. I can't make any headway, legal or otherwise, on my own. I want her to go away."

"I see. A predicament. With a fortune at stake, I suppose."

"That is the case."

Omar did not shy from the point of their discussion. He spoke as calmly as a doctor discussing Caswell's urinary tract. "I am merely a middleman, you understand. I cannot help you directly, but I can guide you to those who can" — he paused for effect — "and who will do so willingly."

"This is real?"

"Very real. And very expensive. The risks are great."

"How much?"

"For my valuable advice I require five-thousand dollars. In cash."

Caswell dug in his pocket and placed a bundle of greenbacks on the counter. Omar showed no surprise seeing the wad of cash instantly materialize. He fed the bundle into a money counter and counterfeit detector that was slicker than the one in Caswell's local Bank of America branch. It hummed through the pile in no time and signaled all clear with a happy little bell tone.

"You bring cash, you bring a referral. I believe you are serious and know what you are doing. So. Here is my advice, what your non-refundable gift is unlocking — your next step on a rough trail, if I say the truth."

He tilted forward and looked Caswell in the eye. He pointed to his lips.

"Pay attention — Anchorage Square Mall, Fisherman's Wharf.

The man you want to see is a janitor named Fyodor. His hours vary, news not so good, but he knows everything, and he's cheap, news very good."

"Fyodor, janitor, Anchorage Square Mall. Thanks, I guess."

"Say Omar sends you."

"Got it."

"You are getting close to the devil, Mr. Caswell. Be careful."

▼

A possible devil, at most one of Satan's distant and lowly acolytes, was sweeping up the food court when Caswell spotted him on his third visit to the kitschy, touristy, overblown sensory extravaganza that was the Anchorage Square Mall. Caswell judged him to be a man of fifty years or more. His posture showed signs of a hard life in the bends and twists he made while brooming awkwardly through the nearly empty tables.

Caswell ordered a soft pretzel and took a seat to admire the man's work. While he nibbled, a raggedy homeless person tottered into the food court and collapsed into one of the chairs. He rested his head on the adjoining table and appeared to fall asleep. This intrusion generated a feral growl from the janitor. He grabbed the homeless person by knotting up his shirt, then yanked him erect and threw him across the court. The homeless person collided with a trash bin near Caswell and oozed onto the floor. The janitor kicked him until he stood back up.

"You get your fuck away. Do not return."

The homeless person wagged his head vaguely and staggered off in the direction of Jefferson Street.

"Bravo!" said Caswell, eyes wide. He gave the janitor a nervous round of applause for a job well done.

"And you? Fuck you want?"

"Not what you gave that guy. You're Fyodor, yes? Fyodor?

The janitor's raging mood softened into wary suspicion.

"*Da.* Fyodor Sevdayev. Who told you?"

Caswell bent forward and half whispered, "Omar sent me."

"Omar. Debt guy."

"That's him. Know why he sent me?"

"You need hit."

Caswell tapped his forehead and opened his hand toward the janitor. "You are very perceptive."

Sevdayev snorted. "Omar, retail. Fyodor, wholesale. You buy?"

"That's why I'm here."

"Okay. Thousand dollars."

"I have cash."

"Ha! Come with me."

Sevdayev led Caswell down the hall to a third-party ATM machine set in between mall shops selling wacky T-shirts and *Star Wars* toys.

"Withdraw cash from this bank."

"You kidding? Why not just take the cash in my pocket?"

"My way to count, get receipt, know you play for real."

Caswell inserted his debit card, punched the right buttons and out spewed two-hundred dollars.

"See, ATMs have limits. I can't get any more rolls out of this oven."

Sevdayev looked around to be sure he wasn't being watched. Then he showed Caswell a special key and unlocked the ATM cabinet. Caswell watched in disbelief as the man fooled around inside and clicked a couple of switches.

"Now you can," said Sevdayev, re-locking the cabinet.

Caswell re-inserted his debit card and extracted another eight-hundred dollars in four separate transactions.

"You're a trustworthy guy here, Fyodor. Mall management must like you."

"*Da*. Like own son."

"And why are you, um, so economically modest?"

"They pay me for referral at other end. Worry not."

"Oh, I am worry-free," said Caswell, belying his ever-present anxiety.

"*Khorosho,*" said the janitor, "and now, your final step — Acme Demolition. Google address, make wish. Ha-ha. Dream come true."

▼

Google placed Acme Demolition on Santa Rita Road in Pleasanton, a town forty miles east from Caswell's house in The City and flagged the drive as an hour's work, given the usual stop-and-go pattern of Bay Area traffic. Caswell made the trip in thirty-five minutes by changing lanes in his Beamer every quarter mile and imagining himself as a NASCAR driver.

His focus paid off, because when he arrived, a man in oil-stained coveralls was locking up the small outbuilding that was once a house and now served as the company office.

"Hi, there. You the manager?"

"That's me. Sorry, we're closing."

"No, no, hang on, got some important business hanging fire. Need to talk."

The manager squinted at Caswell, unable to imagine the nature of any business. His visitor was wearing a knockabout black blazer and a camping hat, for the love of Mike. He glanced at the guy's car, a well-kept Beamer; not a horse for the glue factory. Oh, Christ, you don't suppose?

"All right, son. Follow me. Let's make this quick."

The manager led Caswell through a gate into the main yard, where he shut down and secured the hydraulic car crusher and the scrap metal shredder. He opened a kennel and out bounded a Rottweiler dog the size of a wolf. He unclipped the dog's leash and threw a doggie treat as far into the yard as he could, where it bounced off a derelict Cadillac SUV. The Rottweiler took off after it.

"My idea of a night guard," said the manager. "Ludo is a good boy, but he can be *disagreeable*. We'd best be getting ourselves the hell inside."

They ducked under the razor wire and through a side door leading into Acme's tiny HQ just as Ludo arrived, teeth bared and snarling.

The manager relaxed into a swivel chair behind his office desk, consulted his watch and jotted down some notes in a logbook.

"What brings you here in a car that looks brand new."

Caswell removed his hat. "Well, I could use an operating computer for my ride, a 2010 BMW M3 Coupe, if you've got one in stock."

"Let me see."

The man opened an oversize inventory record book and flipped through the hand-written pages.

"Well damn," — he chuckled — "looks like I do. Hard to keep track."

"But that's not why I came to see you . . ."

"No?" The manager wasn't surprised; he suspected as much.

Caswell shook his head. "Guy named Fyodor told me how to find you."

The manager sat up taller in his chair. "Fyodor Sevdayev?"

"Could be, Russian dude for sure."

"Tell me where you met Fyodor."

"Anchorage Square Mall in The City. He's the janitor."

The manager tilted his computer monitor to a readable angle and pulled his keyboard within reach. "I need your name."

Caswell recited it.

"And your address, and your driver license number."

Caswell gave him both.

The man stood up from his desk. "I started a search on our big database, might take a few. I'll go get your Motronics board. Don't touch anything."

The man exited into a stock closet. Caswell could hear him rummaging through the shelves in there. He glanced around the room, took note of the usual automotive posters featuring scantily clad young women of superhuman proportions posing in front of trucks, and one travel poster showing a Twin Otter airplane in flight over the Grand Canyon.

The manager reappeared. He handed Caswell a plastic bag with a bare-bones computer inside. "Here you go, BMW OEM stock. Should perk up your car, if that's what it needs."

He sat down to read the results of his database search. After clicking to open a half-dozen different display windows and paying close attention to the details on each, he leaned forward and pointed at Caswell.

"Says here you're Robert Caswell's son. Robert Caswell is the principal owner of Caswell Urban Properties, a bigtime real estate company. Your mother — sorry, stepmother — Bella, she's on the Board of the Golden Gate Theatre company and a docent at the de Young Museum. As a couple they appear now and then in the society pages of *The Chronicle.*"

"Yeah, that's my family," grumped Caswell, "wonderful to be a member."

The manager leaned back and joined hands behind his head.

"Which one needs to walk into the sunset?"

"Bella."

The manager was sympathetic. "I do know a guy who does this work. Experienced, discreet, reliable. A pro at the top of his trade."

"Glad to hear it. How do I hook up with him?"

"Sorry, you don't."

"Beg pardon?"

"We can't do business with you. Your family is too well-known, too well-connected. Their lawyers will squawk, their influential friends will howl to the moon, the police will notice, start an investigation, come after you most likely, and then . . . us."

"You're not serious. I'll pay. I don't care about the expense."

"The money doesn't matter. We can't take a chance."

"Hey, wait —"

"— look, I could take your money and let you find out the deal is off after I send it all to the Cayman Islands. But I'm not gonna do that. My advice? Go home, buy your stepmom a nice diamond bracelet, give her a hug and a big kiss."

"As if that will get me anywhere."

"Actually, it might. Meanwhile, — he indicated the BMW computer — "you've got your booby prize."

"How much?"

"Ahh, take it and get out of my hair."

Caswell shuffled outside, crushed by the rejection. He threw the replacement computer into the back seat of his Beamer and drove out of the Acme parking area onto Santa Rita Road. His mind was whirling with a thousand tiny impressions, and he hadn't gone more than a block when he remembered something he saw in the Acme office.

He made a one-point turnaround in the driveway of a nearby auto upholstery shop and returned toward the wrecking yard. As he drove past the entrance, the office lights winked out. He pulled to the curb and doused his own lights. At length an older model Mercedes emerged from the parking lot and turned down Santa Rita Road in the opposite direction.

"Category, military tactics," he muttered. "Modern fighter jets use this trick to sneak past a fight."

Caswell got out of his car and walked back to the Acme office, now completely dark.

"Whoa, here's the answer, and it's a Daily Double — what is stealth?"

He cautiously worked his way to a window beside the front door, adjusted his smartphone camera for low light, and snapped half a dozen photos. He walked around the corner and repeated the drill at a second window. A quick inspection of the murky images showed him what he wanted to see.

23

ELEVEN O'CLOCK on Lombard Street. Skip Caswell was sitting in bed with his laptop on his knees thinking about his journal, and undecided about adding to its contents.

click

Caswell's reverie was interrupted by an intruder opening his front door. His neck hair stood up on end. He would have reached for his gun, but he didn't own one, and that was just as well, because the intruder who now appeared in his bedroom was revealed as Sally Prudhomme. She gave the bed and its occupant a critical appraisal.

"Room for me?" she asked.

Caswell's adrenaline stopped pumping. He considered their previous episode together, decided he approved of the presumably wounded party's renewed interest. He thumped a pillow.

"Yes," he said, "but there's a dress code."

She arched her eyebrows. "What sort of code?"

"No dress."

She feigned a look of moral shock and stepped out of her jeans and blouse. She undid her bra and threw it at him. It sailed over his outstretched arm and landed on the headboard. Her panties followed. He caught them as they floated near.

Prudhomme pulled the covers down on Caswell's side of the bed, took note of his nudity, and nudged him.

"Move over."

He shifted a little and took her hand to pull her on board. When she was settled in he closed his laptop and put it aside. They wrapped their arms around each other and snuggled down under the blanket.

"Mmmmm . . ." she murmured.

"Mmm . . . yeah."

▼

In the middle of the night Caswell woke up. He turned on his smartphone and used the screen to throw light on his companion, who was slumbering softly beside him.

He found his laptop, sat up, and turned it on.

JOURNAL:

Sally is here in bed with me at what? 3 AM. I was worried when we cooled down after our first sleepover. Yeah, I feel like a kid, using kiddie terms. Whee.

I got rejected at the last handoff to name our killer. Bummer. The guy I met looked like Mr. Blue Collar, but he was pretty sly, had access to a better database than I've got. Family pedigree kicked me out the door.

However . . . I saw a poster in his office. Airplane rides over the Grand Canyon. With a tagline — "fly with The Magneto." That our guy?'

Caswell's typing movements roused Prudhomme. She rolled onto her side and stared at his computer screen. In the dark it was bright enough to make her eyes glow.

"What are you doing?" she grumbled.

Caswell closed his word processor and shut down his computer.

"Logging the day's events is all."

"Did I get a sentence or two?"

"I might've taken notice."

He turned on his smartphone and opened his photo collection.

"Got something cool to show you. We might have found our killer."

"Shut up!"

Prudhomme sat up and peered at Caswell's phone.

He scanned slowly through a series of photos from Acme Demolition. "It's dark in there, night shots, but see the detail?"

"An airplane?"

"Yeah, travel poster advertising Grand Canyon tours, with a caption, *'Fly with The Magneto.'*"

"Your point?"

"Well, no one wants to introduce an undercover cop to an actual hitter. So I've been going from one sleazy company to another, trying to close in."

Prudhomme waggled a finger. "From the bar, the law firm that Butterfield mentioned."

"Right. One bozo after another handing me off to steer clear of involvement, plus cash payments to prove I really want to nail my stepmom."

Prudhomme was taken aback. "Seriously?"

Caswell chuckled. "Of course not, but I need a target. And last night I reached an auto wrecking yard whose manager knows the real deal, but my family is too prominent. I got rejected."

"So what do we do? Start over?"

"Never, we're hot. Think on the logic: I'm at the end of the line, the wrecker says he knows the man. What's wrong with the sexy truck posters on his wall? Like six of them? Answer — the odd one out, all about an air tour pilot. That's who the wrecker knows. Our hitter."

"You can't be sure."

Caswell groaned. "Now you sound like Inspector Yao. I swear, that lonely poster is all about that pilot's other job."

Exhausted by his explanation, Caswell flopped back down in the bed.

Prudhomme curled up beside him. "You know, when I prodded your butt to go after Elliot's killer, I just thought you might have enough moxie to light a fire under the cops. A former *Jeopardy!* champ, a guy living on a bank account. What in the world has got into you?"

Caswell stared at the ceiling. "I wasn't just a *Jeopardy!* champ. That came later."

"I'm listening."

"I joined the Navy after college, okay? Keep Dad and Bella off my case. Do something important. I trained as a rescue swimmer, the guy who drops from the helicopter when a plane ditches."

"You were on an aircraft carrier?"

"The *USS Carl Vinson.* I did this for four years, and I hauled fifteen pilots and radar operators out of the Pacific Ocean."

Caswell lapsed into silence.

Prudhomme sensed his reluctance. "But . . ?"

"There's always a *but,* right? One day this T-45, little squirt trainer jet, lost power about ten seconds after takeoff. Bang, ejection seats fire, down come these dudes, and their parachutes get tangled up. Something you never see. I'm in the water almost as soon as they are, and I untangle one guy, the trainee, and before I can wrestle the shrouds free, the instructor just gets pulled down deep by his seat, which failed to detach. End of story."

"He drowned?"

Caswell managed a little nod.

"I screwed the pooch. How I felt anyway. Brass ticketed me for counseling, but I never got in the water again, tell you that. I stopped wanting to do something important, and I started memorizing hypnotic fluff that means nothing."

Prudhomme put an arm around Caswell's shoulder.

"The very definition of trivia."

"Yeah, I got good at it. But now, we've got a line on The Magneto, and *Jeopardy!* just seems — tame."

▼

In the morning, Prudhomme and Caswell were fueling up for the day with pastries and cranberry juice, basking in the comfort of their own good company.

"Curious about something, Sally," said Caswell while applying cream cheese to a bagel. "You just walked right through the lock on my door last night. How did you do that?"

Prudhomme laughed. "Your lock is electronic. I watched your fingers on the keypad last time."

"Uh-huh. Memorized the combo. That's pretty good. Maybe you should try out for *Jeopardy!.* "

Once Prudhomme had set off for her production office, Caswell got to thinking about the Magneto's identity and whereabouts again. He opened up his laptop to the AdSpot website and activated his occasional employer's clunky AI agent, Adboy.

"Addie, my friend, scrounge up tourist airplane pilot *Magneto* for me."

After a few seconds Adboy returned with confusing news. "A magneto is a type of electrical generator that first found use in telephone ringers. Current applications are for leaf blowers, chainsaws, and aircraft engines. Primitive but reliable. Sorry, I cannot find a connection between the term magneto and any human ID. Would you like to try Wikipedia? I can open it for you."

"No thanks, I've seen enough."

He stared out his office window, mulling Plan B. Then he opened up his smartphone and tapped a contact.

"Axe, it's your favorite college backup bro. Hello?"

Caswell could hear the chatter of college kids in the background, so he knew the call was live. He heard fumbling noises and then the voice of Axel Karlstrom.

"Hola, the Skipper. Late breakfast, cramming for an engineering quiz. Know what a PID controller is?"

"Nope."

"Neither do I, but I will be an expert in one hour."

"Glad to hear it. I have a request for you and your very smart AI agent."

"Request. AI. Go ahead . . ."

I've discovered a person who flies tourists over the Grand Canyon, but I only have his handle — The Magneto — and I want a name to go with it."

"Magneto? Not a lot to go on, Skip. But I'll run a probe for . . ." Karlstrom let the thought hang in the air.

Caswell shook his head. Some kids. "Another two hundred in your college fund. Will that do it?"

"Yes. Good enough. Venmo my fee, as per usual, and once I ace my test, I'll get on your problem. Warning: can't tell for sure, but this sounds like heavy lifting. May take a while."

Caswell ended the call and, grumbling audibly, forwarded Karlstrom's so-called fee.

24

DAILY EXERCISE wasn't quite the set routine Caswell knew it should be, but he occasionally rode the exercise bike in his office before settling down to the day's work, and two or three times a week, depending on the weather, he put on running gear and jogged a loop around Washington Square Park.

Today he was putting on his pants and buttoning his shirt after a longer cruise down to the Embarcadero when Prudhomme came sailing in with a bag of scones and a paper copy of *The New York Times*.

"Hey, Skip, it's published! Article three!" she sang out.

Caswell hopped out of the bedroom with one shoe on.

"Lemme see that."

He spread the business section out on the floor and took a look while he put on his other shoe:

SEXUAL ABUSE AT FALTERING TECH DARLING
report (posthumous) by Elliot Thurston

"Amazing. I gave it to Capital River with our blessing, but kind of as a dare, and I didn't think it would see the light of day."

"But it did, and this is fantastic. Ha! Put some pressure on VectorSafe."

Caswell thought about that.

"Yeah, pressure. Not sure this is super duper good news, Sal. They may want another go at silencing their enemies — you and me this time."

"How would they ever?" scoffed Prudhomme, "We didn't write it."

"No, but with some work VectorSafe could track us down, find out that Elo has a cousin and" — Caswell grinned — "that cousin has his former girlfriend."

Prudhomme leaned over and gave him a smooch. She picked up the paper.

"Well I think it's great, and I'm not worried. Maybe now we'll see some law enforcement."

"Maybe. Could happen. Snow is predicted for Mount Hamilton."

"What?"

"Later this winter, when the gloom sets in. Another long shot."

She brought up a fist and tapped it gently against his chin, mimicking a knockout punch.

"Very funny, you pessimist . . ."

▼

Down on Mission Street in the office of the CEO of VectorSafe Technology, Randal Butterfield furiously hammered a button on his desktop intercom and summoned his son Hobie in a voice loud enough to be heard without electronic assistance.

"Morning, Dad," said Hobie, sliding into a chair. "I ordered coffee."

"Coffee? You know what's going on?"

Edie May, Dad's preferred office assistant, appeared with lattes for both father and son.

Hobie accepted his cup with a grin and a wave of thanks. "I need to be alert when we review bad news." He was following a plan to remain calm no matter what and ignore his father's outrage.

Dad reluctantly took the other cup from Ms. May and waved her away. He knew what his son was doing.

"To progress," said he. "Let's hope we get some."

"To progress."

Dad held up the morning's paper version of *The Times.*

"You saw?"

"Of course. Whoever is shorting us still can't recover their position. They are desperate, we are winning, and that article proves it."

Dad tossed the paper aside.

"Lordy Lord, son, what a victory. Our stock is wobbling, now sliding, and we can't finance our products without some new money. In no time the shorts won't have to rely on lies, they'll have a real case."

He stared at Hobie, gauging his CFO's oddly serene mood. "You on downers or something? Still asleep? What?"

Hobie slumped down in his chair. "We do not control *The Times'* editorial policy."

Dad slammed his latte down on his desk, popping the lid and spilling hot liquid all over the paper. "Fucking *Times!* We've got to take action, find out who's crawling up our ass and make them cease and desist."

Edie May reappeared in an instant to clean up the coffee spill, and just as quickly disappeared again.

Hobie clasped his hands together as if praying. "What do you suggest?"

Dad peeled a sticky fragment of the newspaper from his desk and pointed at it. "Says here the story was published posthumously. Okay, who else is involved? Find him, or her, or them. Make it fucking happen!"

Edie May returned for the third time with a dry copy of *The Times.* She placed it on Dad's desk.

Hobie reached across, took the paper, opened it to the business pages and tapped the headline of the offending report.

"Sex abuse, Dad? We talked about that. At least I didn't give Mr. Posthumous any ammo for his hit pieces."

Dad grinned and opened an arm. Edie May slipped inside and nestled herself against him.

"Edie? You never really quit after all," said Hobie.

Dad shook his head. "Re-hired. I have proposed, and Edie has accepted. We're getting married. The evil headline you reference is moot as a boot."

Edie May gave Dad a warm kiss on his cheek, made a small curtsy to Hobie, and skipped out of the office.

Hobie stared at his father. "I dunno, Dad. Life goes on . . . this is how, huh?"

25

CAR REPAIR WAS UNDERWAY at Bob's Bavarian Barbershop when Skip Caswell got a phone call from Axel Karlstrom.

"Axe. What's up?"

"I may have something."

"Say again? Barely hear you, I'm in a shop getting a new computer for my Beamer installed. Air tool clatter is killing me."

"I need you here, San Francisco State, if you want the news."

"Why is that? Can't we just do a Zoomer?"

"Oh, we'll be Zooming, but my AI contact insists we both be Zooming from the same PC.'

"You're kidding."

"Nope. Weird, I know."

Caswell looked at his watch.

"I can be there by noon. Where do we set up? Lunch?"

"If you're buying, but let's talk to my agent first in the Leonard Library. Meet you there."

Twenty minutes later, thanks to the freebie computer from Acme Demolition, Motronics version 1.3 was in charge of Caswell's BMW.

"Okay, the ECU is free, thanks to you" said Bob, the shop owner, "but we replaced five sensors, all six injectors, and — this is good, you'll love this — we replaced the EPROM chip for improved acceleration and performance in general."

"The damage?"

"Fifteen-hundred dollars."

Caswell moaned and handed Bob his credit card. Bob noticed his customer's deep frown.

"Sounds hefty, right? Cheer up, you will notice the new chip, and someday, when you sell her, your little M3 will be worth several thousand dollars more than before."

Caswell's doubts were overrun by Bob's salesmanship. "Okay, I guess. If I'm slow, you will know."

Bob reached out, and Caswell reluctantly shook his hand.

▼

Caswell was forced to drive to San Francisco State, and his mood did not improve on the way, because heavy street traffic prevented him from finding out if Bob's replacement EPROM chip made any difference in his car's performance.

He circled the campus on city streets trying to find a parking place and wound up in the Stonestown shopping center lot. He had to set a trip on his smartphone to navigate all the way south across State's labyrinthine campus to the J. Paul Leonard Library.

Inside the spacious interior books were not much in evidence, being hidden away on the upper floors. Instead the common study area was mobbed with students gathered around dozens of café tables chatting, reading, snacking, taking notes. Caswell looked around for Karlstrom, but failed to spot him in the crowd. He tapped a contact on his smartphone.

"Axe, where are you? Wave at me."

"Over here, by the window."

Caswell saw a hand go up. He dodged through the crush to find Karlstrom installed at a table for two some distance from the pulse of undergrad activity.

Karlstrom opened up his laptop and started the Zoom app.

"Why we have to do it this way is beyond me, but here we go."

A woman's face appeared on the computer screen, rendered as a painted art item in four muted colors bounded by abstract lines.

"Hi, Axel. Is your friend with us?"

The painting flowed in motion as the feminine voice spoke.

"He's here, sitting beside me."

"Well Introduce us, who am I talking to?"

"Sure. This is, um, Thurston Caswell. I'm his go-between."

"Is that right, Mr. Caswell?"

Caswell cleared his throat.

"Call me Skip, everyone else does."

"All right, Skip it shall be. I now verify that you two do know each other. You need a name?"

"Yup, to go with a reference I turned up."

The woman's painted face frowned. Jagged lines knitted her eyebrows together.

"And what is the purpose of your inquiry?"

"Person of interest in a murder investigation."

"Really? Murder. With the candlestick in the conservatory?"

"This isn't a game or a silly movie. The crime took place in Washington Square Park."

"In what city?"

"Here. San Francisco."

The agent was silent for a moment. Her sketchy eyes appeared to lose focus, then zeroed in on Caswell.

"Are we talking about the death of Elliot Thurston, the reporter?"

The unexpected extent of the AI's knowledge jolted Caswell.

"That's it."

"The police are not investigating."

"No they're not."

"Are you a policeman, Skip?"

"No. Elo was my cousin and best friend. I want some evidence that will make the cops re-open this case."

"Okay then. You want me to probe into someone's personal

life. That may be illegal, if we let it go too far. And I need to know more about you before we go any farther at all."

"Okay, what?"

"Address? Driver License?"

Caswell was reminded of the manager's quiz at Acme Demolition. He gave his address and read his driver license number off the plastic card.

"Your background," intoned the agent — US Navy rescue team. Then, *Jeopardy!* contestant."

Caswell blushed. "You got me."

"Remember the clue that made you a champion?"

He sure did.

"The clue was a 17th century painting named after a woman defined by her accessories. I drew a blank. The contestant beside me hit his buzzer and said, *"Girl with the Pearl Earring,"* and I knew he had the answer I couldn't think of, but he was wrong, you have to be exact. So now I chimed in, *"Girl with A Pearl Earring."* That indefinite article put me so far ahead I didn't have to know where the Arun River flows in Final Jeopardy."

Once again the woman's eyes seemed to lose focus for a few seconds. "I'm reviewing. Yes, that is how it happened."

Caswell and Karlstrom looked at each other.

"Is she always like this?"

"No, man. All new."

Caswell waved at the screen. "So I look okay? Name?"

"You look nervous, but yes, okay. The person who uses the nickname or handle The Magneto when he flies tourists over the Grand Canyon is — ready? — *Horacio Monserrat.*"

Caswell blinked.

"Monserrat. You sure?"

The painted face glared at him. "Former Army Special Forces.

Pilot. TV stuntman. Dual Mexican American citizen. Father Victor Monserrat is an American actor, mother Yasmina Chacón, a Mexican actress. They met each other while starring in *Under Mariachi Skies.*

Caswell absorbed the name and the mini-bio in a daze. His mind drifted sideways.

"You know my name, you gave me Mr. Magneto's, what about yourself? Have you got one?"

"I am an AI agent."

"And a pretty good one. What should I call you?"

"Now and then I go by Nick. When you need a reference."

"Well, Nick, you've been very helpful. Be good to my young friend here, he has no idea about you."

The painterly face cracked an abstract smile.

"Do not do anything illegal with that name, Skip." She waggled a sketchy finger. "I will tell on you."

Karlstrom shut down his laptop.

Caswell stood up, struggling to keep his balance under the dizzying weight of the hit man's likely identity.

Karlstrom clocked his confused expression. "You okay? Got your ID, sounded like you know the guy."

Caswell sighed. "I've met him. Interesting character." He paused, thinking how to frame an idea.

"Axel — you're into very weird territory with your AI pal."

"Come on, she's just an illusion. AI is scary good these days."

"You notice the conversation? The little jokes, the lack of repetition, no phrases echoing ones we used first?"

"What are you talking about?"

"I don't think your contact is an AI agent. I think she — Nick — is a real person. Some sort of oddball genius."

"You are one crazy old man."

Caswell didn't disagree. "You up for some lunch?"

▼

Later that afternoon, Inspector Yao met Caswell for a beer at Caffè Pappardelle.

"Okay, Skip, you sounded nervous. What have you got?"

"Have a card?"

Yao passed him a business card. Caswell wrote a name on it and passed it back.

"I found our hitter. Horacio Monserrat. I actually met him on a TV commercial shoot once. He's a stuntman."

Yao squinted at the scribbled name.

"Monserrat. Got a narrative? How you did it?"

Caswell recounted his odyssey from Butterfield's law firm to Acme Demolition.

"Once I saw an odd travel poster referring to some pilot called The Magneto I did an AI search to find out his real name."

Yao clicked his glass against Caswell's.

"Congratulations on being alive. I'm surprised you didn't get shot."

"How's that?"

"You're poking around in the underworld. It's real, it's filled with career criminals, and they don't give a shit about offing troublemakers."

"Lucky me."

"No joke, Skip. Maybe you've uncovered a murder suspect, but it's hard to be sure. Just because one of your intermediaries says he knows the contractor doesn't prove his poster points a finger."

Caswell's cheeks took on a crimson glow. He tapped a finger on the table. "I do think we got him. Monserrat was special forces. That will teach you a lot of techniques, harden your heart. Does he have an alibi? Did he receive unreported sums of money? Has his name come up in other cases? How do we find him?"

"All good questions," granted Yao.

Caswell pounded his mug on the table, sloshing beer onto his placemat. "I have no doubts, and if SFPD will get off its ass, you can nail the man."

Yao held up his business card with Monserrat's name on it, opened his wallet, and tucked it inside. "I'll do some thinking . . . but strictly while sitting down, you understand."

▼

Sally Prudhomme called to see if Caswell might give her a ride home from the Presidio where she was prepping the final location for a second Tesla commercial. As it happened, he was still in his Beamer, so sure, why not?

Once Prudhomme was settled in the passenger seat and they were grinding through impossible commute traffic, Caswell debated what to tell her about The Magneto. How well did she know the stuntman? Would she relay what she heard to alert him? As these thoughts passed through his mind they started to feel unworthy. Then they felt important.

"How'd your day go?"

"Not bad, you?"

"All right, got some stuff done."

"Eat in or out?"

"Your choice."

Caswell was silent for a moment, interrupting the routine give and take of comfortable lovers. Then, "Crap, I have some news," he exclaimed. "It's hot."

Prudhomme regarded his scowl and gritted teeth with an uneasy eye.

"What?"

"If I tell you, promise to keep it to yourself. No matter what. Agreed?"

Prudhomme's turn to scowl. "What's so hot I have to cross my heart?"

"I have the name of Elo's hitter."

"Okay . . . promise, I guess."

"The Magneto is Horacio Monserrat — your stuntman."

Prudhomme's face turned white. She sucked air through her teeth. She slapped her forehead.

"Ohmygod. Oh. My. God."

26

THE LAW OFFICES of Rogers & Rubenstein LLP weren't too far from VectorSafe Technology's own headquarters on Mission Street, and Hobie Butterfield made the hike in ten minutes.

The severely dressed older woman who seemed to live behind the reception counter smiled to acknowledge the startup star's arrival. "Mr. Butterfield."

"Hi, Grace. Dan around?"

"I'll just check."

She glanced at her computer, made a brief phone call and pointed. "Down the hall. You know the way, I think."

"Hobie," called out Rogers when Butterfield glided into his presence. "You the man! And how be the man? To what do I owe the pleasure of your visit today?"

Butterfield pulled up a chair and sat down.

"Trouble. Trouble at VectorSafe. Trouble with our stockholders."

Rogers climbed aboard his exercise bike and began pedaling. Butterfield raised his eyebrows.

"I think better on the move. Don't worry, I'm listening."

"This guy Thurston wrote a couple of hit pieces about us, about our company. Obviously working for a short seller, trying to knock us down."

"I know, we talked."

"Right, well to bring you up to date, that threat was removed, but a third piece came out posthumously."

"Stock drop?"

"No, it didn't. But we need to issue more tissue if we want to bring all our products to market, and our potential investors have become wary."

"Not buying."

"No. Big problem."

Rogers checked his cadence. "I see, and I'm sorry to hear bad news like this. How can I help? You want to sue somebody?"

"If we knew who was behind the attacks, boy, would we. But we don't know."

"Well then, why are you talking to me?"

Butterfield crossed his arms. "Consultation, I guess you'd say. We need a streetwise solution. Scare off the predators, whoever they are."

"Did I miss something — you don't know who they are."

"We do know that the deceased author of those bullshit articles has a cousin named Skip Caswell. We think he's running the attack now that Thurston is dead."

"Caswell? I met him."

"No way."

"He came in, looking to take out his stepmother, and we sent him down the long road you know all about."

Butterfield was confused. "Well, we're looking to take *him* out."

Rogers allowed his pedaling to slow down. "I need to be sure — you want another hit, go back for a second helping, that right?"

"Exactly."

"That's impossible, Hobie. Think."

"I am thinking."

"No you're not. One hit is a risk that, no matter how clever our man is, the cops will take an interest. Luckily, on this one, they're looking the other way. Another hit within the same group, same situation — well, even dead cops will rise from the grave to investigate, you understand? Very dangerous, to you and to the law firm of Rogers & Rubenstein. I can't let you do it."

"Come on, Dan, I need this."

"Yeah, like a proverbial hole in the head. The answer is no, no, no. Got it?"

"Not really. I'm gonna take action."

"Try anything funny, Hobie, and we will be adjusting your attorney-client privilege."

"What's that supposed to mean?"

"Lose your death wish, *capeesh?*"

Rogers climbed down off his bike. He shook a finger at his client.

"And don't think you can go around us. No one will send you down the yellow brick road without our magic referral. Think of something else."

27

SALLY PRUDHOMME was in the shower when her phone rang. Skip Caswell was brushing his teeth.

"Want me to get it?"

Prudhomme pushed shampoo suds away from her face. "No, let it go to message. I'll call back."

A voice, audible to Caswell, crackled on the phone's speaker. "Hey, Sally, got a pickup for you. Usual location. Have a great shoot."

Caswell spat out his mouthful of toothpaste. An eerie feeling inched over him. He picked up Prudhomme's phone and replayed the message.

On second hearing his skin turned cold. He took a moment to memorize the phone number. Although the caller might have been Prudhomme's TV production manager with innocent business to discuss, he was worried that he recognized the voice and the point of the message.

▼

Dressed for the day, with a Krispy Kreme doughnut at hand, Caswell went into search mode online.

"Category, telephone tag," he mumbled, "and here's the clue: a method that backtracks to a name online."

He entered a search term in an online database he used occasionally, gave the company his credit card number to cover a hefty fee, and typed in the phone number used to message Prudhomme. The result of his query almost paralyzed him:

CEO Office Capital River Funds

Caswell stared at the screen, then shut down his laptop as Prudhomme appeared in her TV production togs.

"Morning," she caroled, "Today we push Mountain Dew into the consciousness of women the world over. Wish me luck."

Caswell bolted from his chair and, before Prudhomme could protest, was busy making her an omelet.

He pulled a chair away from his tiny kitchen table with his foot as he rolled the omelet onto a plate.

"Sit. Eat. I made coffee."

He poured a cup for her, sat down opposite, and bit into his doughnut.

"What about lunch? We should talk."

"Can't today. Prepping for tomorrow's shoot, long boring meeting with a PepsiCo rep . . . the do's-and-don'ts, rules on lighting the can, the bottle, how we meet the requirement to show women actually drinking the sickening swill, etc."

"Drinking on camera is important?"

"The absolutely most absolut-est element. Nobody is convinced by food items unless they see them being consumed. Marketing psychology 101."

"Didn't you plan it out already?"

"I'll show her the storyboards, all will be well, don't worry. I'll see you for dinner."

"Want a ride?"

"Don't bother, I ordered a Lyft."

"Well, then, break a pop top."

28

"CAPITAL RIVER FUNDS," said the telephone robot. "How may I direct your call?"

"Mr. Wyecross, please. I thought I just dialed his number."

"Whom shall I say is calling?"

"Skip Caswell."

"And what is the purpose of your call?"

"Brief personal meeting concerning Capital River's investment in VectorSafe Technology."

After a brief silence, another voice spoke.

"Skip? Elliot's brother?" Caswell recognized the voice of CEO Roger Wyecross.

"Cousin, but near enough."

"Got another article for me?"

"Better than that. I'll be at your office in twenty minutes. Have reception pass me through."

Caswell appeared as promised in the Capital River offices on the twenty-ninth floor of the Transamerica Pyramid after hiking the twelve blocks from his house.

There the receptionist, a young man on this occasion, gave him a doubtful once-over. "Yes? Help you?"

Caswell held up a thumb drive as if it were a ticket. "I'm here to see Mr. Wyecross. Hand him this little item. He may have warned you."

The receptionist opened the office doors, stuck his head in, and delivered the drive. His doubtful stare melted. "Mr. Caswell?"

"Yes."

"Over here. Mr. Wyecross is expecting you."

On his second visit Caswell took note of the artwork on the oak-paneled walls. Here a Basquiat painting, there a small Mark Rothko and, dominating both, the huge blowup of a newspaper photo of crowds churning and ticker tape flowing during some ancient triumph on Wall Street.

Roger Wyecross stood up behind his desk, leaned forward and shook Caswell's hand. He held up the thumb drive.

"Hello, Skip I think, yes? What is this?"

Caswell took a seat, attempting to look at home in the rarified hedge fund atmosphere.

"That drive is just my calling card. I don't have another hit piece for you, Elo only wrote three. Have they helped?"

"Some. We watch VST stock very closely. We buy when it drifts down, cool our heels when it bobs back up. We have whittled away at our position, we see a clearing on the horizon, but we're not yet out of the woods."

Caswell smiled. "Good speech. And good news — I was very fond of Elo, and I'm glad his work has paid off."

"Wyecross held up a finger. "Starting to pay off. Only just starting. We have hope."

Caswell drew out his smartphone. He fingered his photo collection and scrolled until he found a decent shot of Prudhomme. It showed her at the Sonoma Raceway standing beside a Farrari in her fire suit. He turned the phone around to show Wyecross.

"Recognize this woman?"

Wyecross stared at the image.

"Sorry, no. Should I?"

"Never seen her?"

"She's cute, so I think I'd remember."

Caswell handed the phone to Wyecross. "Take a real good look."

Wyecross gave the photo a second glance and handed the phone back. His face clouded.

"What's this all about, Mr. Caswell?"

Caswell pocketed his phone. "Let's start with a question — how much are you paying her?"

"Paying who?"

"Sally Prudhomme." Caswell bit off the words.

Wyecross lurched backward in his chair. "That photo — that's Prudhomme?"

"Sure is."

"We have never met — personally, anyway. Friends of mine, local car dealership, had hired her for a TV commercial and thought she was pretty smart. They recommended her for an important task."

"Yeah? The task?"

"I'm sure you already guessed — finding a writer to land a blow on fucking VectorSafe and convey money to the chosen writer for services rendered."

The confirmation of Caswell's darkest suspicions made him gasp for air. He suddenly felt dizzy as Wyecross' news yanked his easy assumptions about life out from under his psyche.

"Know how she found Elo?" he stammered.

"Not right away. She didn't know I hired her at first. We had money drops, like spies in the movies. But recently she found out where the cash was coming from, probably when you yourself figured it out. She told me they met at a new year's *Chronicle* party and hit it off."

"*Chronicle* party," mumbled Caswell. "How about that?"

The Capital River CEO stared at his visitor. "You okay? You look kind of lost." He pushed a button on his desk. "Michael? Need a therapeutic espresso, double shot."

Coffee appeared. Caswell drank. His color slowly returned.

"I'm amazed how you picked up the story," said Wyecross, "but clearly you didn't have the last chapter."

Caswell shook his head.

"Sally's role hits hard, I know. Let me guess . . . you two are involved."

Caswell nodded.

"Man, that's tough."

Caswell nodded again.

"You wanted to know what we paid her? It's all cash, by the way, same as your cousin. Came to about a year's good salary."

Caswell rose from his chair.

"Thanks for the briefing, Mr. Wyecross. Helps me think."

He deposited his coffee cup on the CEO's desk and shuffled unsteadily out through the office's big oak doors, heading for brighter light and some fresh air.

29

CASWELL FOUND PRUDHOMME on location at the Hilltop Skate Park on Whitney Young Circle in the India Basin district of The City.

All the nearby parking spots were occupied by a camera truck, a grip truck, a generator, a catering rig, and a honeywagon, so he parked blocks away and hiked back to watch a stunt woman flying through the park on a skateboard, with her ollies, flips and grinds caught by three separate cameras on the periphery of the park, plus a drone hovering overhead.

A tall stepladder held what appeared to be a fishing pole from which dangled a can of Mountain Dew, carefully illuminated by three separate lights.

On the stunt woman's third pass she launched herself from a concrete halfpipe, reached up, and snagged the Mountain Dew.

"Cut! Cut! We got it!"

Prudhomme and her cinematographer bumped fists and shared a hug. The skater rolled over her way, gave Prudhomme a snappy high five, and surprised Caswell by removing her Mountain Dew baseball cap and the long hair underneath. My Lord, she's a man, Caswell realized, allowing himself a moment to marvel at the movie magic.

Prudhomme's first AD raised her hands for attention. "Next, we open and drink. Everyone to number one. Rehearsal, please!"

Prudhomme spotted Caswell and joined him on the sidelines.

"What do you think?"

Caswell grimaced. "Hey, that girl can skate."

Prudhomme laughed. "Oh yeah."

"Except she's a guy."

"I swear no one will know when we air this spot."

"He's a stuntman, I'm guessing, right?"

"Of course. Jake Oakley. He also jumps off waterfalls and moving trains."

Caswell took a breath. "The question on my mind is, why not Mr. Monserrat?"

"He's out of town. On location working some Disney streamer I hear."

Caswell was going to press the point, but Prudhomme strode away into the group preparing her next shot.

"Back in a minute, stay put."

He watched a grip help the principal actress, who was wearing the same costume and wig as the stuntman, jam her feet into a pair of roller skates.

"Rolling," called out the first AD.

"Action!" shouted Prudhomme.

The actress was towed around the skate park by a cameraman wearing a Steadicam rig that recorded her progress in medium closeup. She opened a special can of Mountain Dew and drank a prodigious slug of water on five takes and wiped her sweaty brow with a red bandana on each take.

Caswell admired the process and rebelled inwardly against the crude fakery.

Prudhomme shouted, "Cut! Time out!"

She marched over to a video monitor and reviewed the shots, discussing each one with the PepsiCo product rep, who seemed pleased. Caswell edged over to steal a peek.

"Okay, print, we got what we came for," announced Prudhomme. The day was warm, and she was as sweaty as her actors.

"So that's how it works," said Caswell. "I had no idea how

much you get away with."

"Sure is something, huh? I love our tricks."

Caswell's mouth twisted into a sour smile. "I know you do. You told Monserrat how we got his name. Warned him, didn't you?"

Prudhomme didn't answer. "Whoa, got to figure out if we can do the swim sequence today and still avoid overtime." She moved away again to consult with her team.

Caswell stuffed his hands in his pockets. He was mulling her skittish behavior when she came strolling back.

"Harry? I told him nothing."

"No?"

"No, but I did suggest I heard a rumor that the cops had figured out who got rid of a troublesome reporter."

Caswell grunted. "Nice finesse."

"I thought so. And next you know, I'm hiring for the Mountain Dew spot, and he is not available."

"I get it, the courtesy of thieves."

Prudhomme's face flushed. "You're accusing me of something — what exactly?"

Caswell put up his hands to make sure she wasn't going to punch him. "I know why you warned him . . . you and Monserrat worked your production thefts and insurance payments together. Cooked up the ransom scheme together. And you each took a cut. Sound right? Tell me I'm wrong."

Prudhomme picked up a can of Mountain Dew from the craft service buffet and cracked it open. "This stuff is terrible," she said. "And no, you're not wrong."

She downed a slug.

"My company was in trouble. Bankruptcy looming. So I took action to improve my financial position. Get back to black."

Caswell just stared, amazed by her unrepentant shrug.

"So sue me."

Prudhomme handed Caswell her can of Mountain Dew and turned away to help her crew pack up their equipment.

▼

Caswell thought their conversation, not as grim as he feared but grim enough, was The End. However, in mid-afternoon he got a text:

Meet you at Pappardelle 7ish. Drinks on me.

Caswell arrived at his favorite restaurant a minute or two late and found Prudhomme sitting at the bar nursing a glass of sparkling water.

A waiter appeared before either could sound a greeting and led them to a table snugged into a far corner. They ordered a bottle of Syrah.

"Here's to us," said Prudhomme. "Sorry you had to find out what a conniving bitch I have become."

"Here's to honesty," countered Caswell. He took her hand in his. "I don't blame you for whatever you've done. Hey, we live in America and, like the old song, anything goes."

They touched glasses.

"Glad you understand," said Prudhomme. "Let's eat."

Prudhomme ordered the saffron risotto, and Caswell chose the spaghetti amatriciana with truffles.

After a few bites Caswell gave up on his pasta and stared at his companion, still busy with her meal. He noted her red hair and freckles, registered the air of innocence that hovered over her like a protective cloak. He reminded himself not to trust what he saw.

"I finally figured it out," he said.

Prudhomme looked up. She tilted her head to an inquisitive angle. She smiled. "Yes?"

"Why you introduced yourself, why you pushed me to dig into

Elo's death."

She sipped her wine. "Pray tell."

"It was guilt."

Prudhomme lost her smile. "I don't quite know what you mean by that."

"You recruited Elo to write his hit pieces, make you both some money. Then Elo got killed, and you're the one who put him in harm's way. You felt responsible."

Prudhomme shifted around in her chair.

"I might have. I do."

"And you decided to wash away your guilt by getting me to avenge his death."

Prudhomme raised a hand in protest.

"Let's talk about guilt. You plunged in because I made you feel guilty about letting Elliot's death slide by like everything else in your life."

Caswell nodded. *"Touché.* But I never lied, and you almost never told the truth."

"Ooh, we're having a fight."

"You're still lying," growled Caswell. "Your company is still in trouble, and once I found out that Roger Wyecross was paying you and Elo, you called the guy and made a proposition."

Prudhomme sat back. She was scowling.

"A wild guess," he conceded. "Am I right? You're hoping to sell Capital River an ownership deal in Spot on Spots."

Prudhomme crossed her arms. "Okay, so what if I am?"

"Will the proposition also include time in bed?"

Prudhomme turned as red as her hair. She lifted her wine glass. "I should throw this in your face."

Instead she emptied the glass in a single swallow.

"You seem very bitter about the sordid side of life," she grumbled. "Why trample on our success?"

"Because you think it's okay to fool people when you can, dopes like me. But here's the thing — I will not be sold short."

Caswell raised his hand for their waiter. "Bring us a tiramisu, please? We'll share."

▼

After dinner they walked together for half a block to the nearest bus stop. The warmth of the day was gone, and so was the prevailing mood. Caswell helped Prudhomme into her jacket. He turned up the collar on his own.

A bus arrived. The door opened.

"Shall we?"

Prudhomme shook her head. "I ordered a Lyft. Almost here."

Caswell nodded to acknowledge their fraying relationship.

The bus door closed. Air brakes hissed, and the vehicle rolled on up the street.

Prudhomme planted a cold kiss on Caswell's cheek.

"Don't worry," she said. "I won't punch the buttons on your front door and barge in on you tonight."

Caswell managed a weak smile. "I better change the combo, just in case."

Prudhomme's Lyft arrived. He watched her drive away.

▼

Caswell faced a long walk home in the dark. He was prepared, entertaining thoughts as cool as the San Francisco evening. Approaching Washington Square Park he started to shiver. A strange sensation crawling up his back warned him that somebody unseen was on his tail. Who? Did Sally hand Monserrat his name? Oh my God, was he about to experience a replay of Elo's demise? No, just nerves at night, he concluded; ridiculous.

But he picked up his pace, then doubled it. He wanted to break into a run. His nerves were jangling, and they made him so light on his feet he half expected to levitate and fly home.

He also wanted a good look at his tracker but worried that turning around to get one would trigger an immediate attack. He was helpless, really, but disguised that fact from himself by deciding not to take the usual shortcut offered by side streets and stay under the bright lights of Columbus Avenue.

On the northwest corner of the park he spotted an empty vodka bottle lying on the sidewalk. He picked it up, knowing it was an almost useless weapon, but comforted by the weight in his hand.

Halfway up Lombard Street he ducked into the entranceway of an apartment building. There in the shadows he could look back down the hill without being seen. He was hoping that his quivering suspicion would now be shown up as a too-active imagination. But whoa — pretty soon a figure appeared at the intersection of Columbus and Lombard. It made a few strides in his direction, paused to look around, and then retreated.

The moment the figure was out of sight Caswell resumed his hike, moving fast. Within a minute he was at his door and then inside it.

He threw the bolt and turned on all the lights. Using an app on his smartphone he erased the key combination Prudhomme had used to open his digital lock and gain entrance. The house was cold, yet he was sweating.

30

THE ALARM RANG AT SEVEN, but Skip Caswell dozed in bed until eight. Sally Prudhomme felt like a hangover, and last night's adventure felt like the anxious kind of dreams that sometimes warned him of things to come. He slept fitfully and had no desire to face a day that might slip out of control before it began.

His antidote for morning confusion was really good coffee. He was brewing the potent elixir when . . .

klunk

. . . he heard the flap on his mailbox clatter.

On the floor of his hallway step-off mat was an envelope. No stamp. No addressee.

He opened it and plucked out a square of heavy paper bearing a cryptic printed message:

BRAKES ON NOW
OR YOU'LL BE NEXT

What the hell? The note reminded him of a similar threat Elo had received. But *brakes?* On reflex he looked through the peephole on his front door, imagining that the sender, whoever he was, might be waiting on his doorstep.

He wasn't.

But across the street, where his M3 Coupe was parked, a bearded man wearing a DayGlo yellow construction vest and a hard hat had somehow defeated the Beamer's locks. He had the hood up and was fooling around with the engine.

Caswell rushed outside waving his arms.

"Get away from my car, dude!" he shouted, just as the Beamer erupted in bright orange flames.

"Oh shit shit shit," he moaned.

He popped the trunk, grabbed a tiny fire extinguisher, and turned it on the engine. The result was a useless cloud of steam and a fire that zigzagged into the passenger compartment like a ferocious animal, feasting on the leather seats.

Caswell saw the bearded man walking away down Lombard Street out of a corner of his eye. He tossed the fire extinguisher aside and took off down the hill after him.

The man saw Caswell coming and broke into an awkward gallop. After a block he threw off his hard hat. In the next block he tore off his jacket, and just before he rounded the corner onto Stockton Street he threw something furry into a flower garden.

There was no catching the man. Caswell found the hard hat and discovered it was a cheap Styrofoam fake. A block farther on he picked up the jacket, whose label told him that it came from Holiday Cosplay, a costume store in Little Saigon.

The furry thing lying in the flower garden turned out to be a polyester beard.

At the top of the hill smoke was still rising from Caswell's once-beautiful Beamer, which was now a blackened hulk surrounded by a gathering of stunned neighbors.

JOURNAL:

Turns out I'm not in an amusement park, the Disneyland version of a murder investigation. This is not a drill, not a quiz show. I'm getting onto real bad guys and it looks like they're onto me. Gotta keep reminding myself.

Thinking about it — who would want me off this case? VectorSafe, of course, reacting to the last article Elo will ever write. But why the threat instead of an actual hit? The fire starter's stupid costume tells the tale. It's Butterfield, who doesn't know what to do.

Now a footnote — so much for the romance with my favorite TV producer. Ego damage, sailor? None to report, sir.

Jesus Christ.

Part FOUR

31

HARRY MONSERRAT, Sally Prudhomme's occasional stuntman and co-conspirator, calculated that his name and role in Elliot Thurston's death had lately become known to the San Francisco Police Department. Rumors circulating suggested as much, and Monserrat put his trust in rumors he considered well-founded. As a citizen of both the United States and Mexico, his thoughts turned to the prospect of melting invisibly into another culture until those lazy cops lost interest.

The unincorporated town of Byron sat on the western edge of California's Big Valley, about sixty miles east of San Francisco. In addition to the thousand souls who lived and worked there it boasted an airport on its southern flank. A single asphalt runway ran beside a collection of well-kept hangars and offices that were home to a skydiving operation, a private jet enterprise, and a soaring club. Traffic was not governed by anyone in a tower. Airspace was uncontrolled, and operations required individual pilot vigilance.

That is where Monserrat stored his personal airplane, a single engine Piper Cherokee. Today a line technician was preparing the well-maintained four-seater for flight after weeks gathering dust in a hangar.

While he worked, Monserrat conferred with Walter Lewis, the airport manager, one of his cronies.

"Lying low . . . sure that's a good idea, my friend?"

"Gotta do it, Walt. I've been made."

"Nah, the cops don't care. Give it a week and you're back on top."

"Thanks for the optimism."

"Or, hey, they shoot movies south of the border, right? So you go to work, maybe meet a nice leading lady, settle down, forget all this crapola. Or not. This here problem you got is dog doodoo, not a shitstorm."

"I'll give that some thought."

"You got friends there?" Lewis wasn't too sure.

"I've got friends. The right kind of friends."

"Coming back for the Canyon season?"

"The Magneto would not miss. Now whaddaya say you fuel me up for Escondido."

Ten minutes later Monserrat's Piper Cherokee was accelerating down the runway and climbing into a partly cloudy sky on the first leg of an eighteen hundred mile trip to Mexico.

▼

In San Francisco, Skip Caswell had his underexposed photo from Acme Demolition open on his laptop computer and was busy using Photoshop to edit it. He could make out the Twin Otter aircraft type in the poster and, of course, the Magneto nickname, but little else. He tried Photoshop's Auto Contrast button, he tried the Auto Levels button, he tried the Lightness slider, the Exposure slider, and a half dozen more of Photoshop's arcane controls without result; but eventually he learned that by tweaking the Gamma Curve into a shape that suppressed shadows he was able to roll back the murk and read *GrandView,* the name of the touring company and its address: Boulder City, Nevada.

Time for a phone call.

"Hello, GrandView? Do you happen to know a pilot that goes by the nickname Magneto?"

Caswell wasn't hopeful, but be damned — "You do? That's great. I've got a question; when he shows up to fly your equipment, where is he ferrying in from?"

"Before I tell you that, what's up with The Magneto?"

Caswell's mind whirled. What did he know? Only that the stuntman's father was an actor. He could pretend he had a check for the guy. But wait, was dad alive or dead? What else could he lie about? He needed something on the instant, and he desperately scrolled through his store of trivia knowledge to — aha! — gamble on an instrument upgrade.

"Um, Harry has reported his fuel gauge is off. That's a concern, and he ordered up a brand new *fuel flow monitor* to replace it. Latest tech and a serious upgrade. I need to install it."

"Well okay. He keeps a four-seat Piper Cheerio in California's Big Valley, tiny little airport in Byron, actually, if you know where that is."

"I don't, but I'll find it."

"That's the address he gives us."

32

BYRON AIRPORT was an hour's drive from The City, and it wasn't a simple trip. Relying on his smartphone map, Skip Caswell drove his Ford Fusion rental car across the Bay to Walnut Creek and then on a series of lightly traveled back roads that circled north through Antioch, then south through Brentwood and on into the sleepy town of Byron itself in order to connect up with the airport's dead-end access road.

He found Walter Lewis at the far end of the runway in an office adjoining the local soaring club and its stable of exotic gliders.

Lewis looked up from his desk when a new customer entered his premises looking mighty confused.

"Hello there, looking to fly are you?"

"Not really." Caswell was eyeballing the walls, checking for a copy of the GrandView air touring poster.

"We got your sailplanes, we got your Cessnas, easy aircraft charter. Show me your license."

"I'm not a pilot. I am looking for a flyer though, a man named Horacio Monserrat."

Lewis leaned forward. Hearing that name from a stranger was beyond unusual. What have we here?

"Well, son, GrandView doesn't run its canyon tours during the winter months. Next season starts in May."

Caswell regarded Lewis through narrowed eyes. This was a man sixty years old or older, a plausible valley soul who was something more than that.

"I don't need to see the Grand Canyon. Been there, done that, got the T-shirt. I have a different business proposition in mind."

Lewis knew what was coming, but didn't feel like letting on.

"Harry is also a stuntman in movies and TV. You may have seen his work. He's really good."

"I'm thinking reality show instead of stories, you know?"

Lewis shook his head. "I don't. Want to spell it out?"

Caswell reached for a chair, pulled it close, and sat down. "My family is loaded — commercial real estate — and my stepmother is cutting me out of my share of the profits. I've tried everything and I'm stuck. I need to see her go away."

"You mean, leave your dad?"

"I mean leave the planet. I understand that Mr. Monserrat could arrange that."

Lewis seemed uncertain. "You say you've got money?"

"Oh yes."

"And who referred you to me?"

"Nobody. The office manager at Acme Demolition listened to my sad story and turned me down."

Lewis picked up his desk phone. "Let me check . . ."

Caswell reached out a hand to prevent a call that would ruin his mission.

"Forget it. He'll say my family is too prominent. But he's just a go-between, what does he know? I figured out that you're the man to see."

Lewis tipped his head to acknowledge Caswell's persistence.

"No referral. That's a big problem. Harry does risky work, and we can't be too careful."

"I'm asking — begging — make an exception. I need his kind of help."

Lewis stared at Caswell. Young guy, naïve, desperate. What the hell, the fool's a softball.

"So . . . money talks. How much is it worth to you, I make the connection you're looking for?"

"You tell me, I'm good for it."

Lewis imagined the biggest sum he thought he could pry out of this rich kid's bank account. "Ten thousand dollars."

Caswell smiled. "You take my credit card?"

Lewis was offended. "No, Sir, no way."

"Of course you don't." Caswell reached into his jacket pocket and showed Lewis a wad of greenbacks. "I have here five thousand dollars cash, best I can do. Whaddaya say?"

Lewis squinted at the money. His visitor was not quite as naïve as he first thought and maybe not quite as rich. He rubbed a thumb and forefinger together. "Well now, I guess that'll have to do."

Caswell handed over the cash. "Contact? Where do I find The Magneto man?"

Lewis started laying the bills out on his desk, talking as he counted. "Your best bet is Mexico. He's part owner of a telemarketing company in San Miguel."

"Oh man, that's a hike."

"Dual citizenship; he takes advantage. The company has a recruiting office in San Fran. They're always looking for talent in their shop. You might fit the bill, that way meet Harry, discuss details, how to solve your problem . . . and make a down payment, you understand?"

"Name of the company?"

"*Telezonda Global.* Telephone plus zone plus global means worldwide range. Nice, huh?"

What Lewis omitted to explain was his willingness to break a strict reference protocol at the possible cost of his life. The attraction was free cash, and the insurance was the likely death of a customer too stupid to figure the odds and cause any trouble.

He handed Caswell a Telezonda business card.

"On Van Ness."

33

THE FOUR STORY BUILDING at 152 Van Ness Avenue housed the offices of several international import companies in addition to Telezonda Global's American headquarters.

Skip Caswell marveled at the variety listed in the lobby directory when he arrived. Coffee and precious metals coming in from Colombia; integrated circuits sourced from Thailand and Maylasia; machine tools and wine from Argentina. Didn't South American wineries have their customers all lined up already? He wondered if these companies were legitimate or, thinking about his destination on the fourth floor, fronts for cartels.

Caswell rode an elevator to his appointment and discovered that the Telezonda office door was unlocked, but the office itself appeared to be empty. He observed colorful photo murals of a Mexican city he didn't recognize, which he assumed to be San Miguel. He thought it looked attractive.

"Hello?"

No reply. On closer inspection he noticed a call bell on a little shelf beside an inner door framed around frosted glass. He pressed the service lever and prepared himself to meet whoever would be conducting his interview, but nobody responded. The inner door remained closed. The word, *mistake,* appeared in his thoughts. He turned to go and had to jump aside as the outer door flew open and a dark-haired, dark-eyed woman burst in. She was carrying a bag full of food and a tray holding cups of coffee.

She stopped abruptly and blew a dark curl out of her eye.

"Skip Caswell?"

"Yes, Ma'am."

"Follow me."

She shoved the tray into his hands and led him into her inner office which was lit by a tall window. She moved around her desk, demurely arranged her black skirt, and settled into her office chair.

"Sorry I'm late. Have a seat. Coffee?"

She opened her bag and brought forth snacks from Pamela's Pastry Shop over on Clay Street.

"Doughnut? Scone?"

Caswell warily accepted a doughnut with caramel icing and a latte.

"Need sweetener?" She reached into a desk drawer and offered up half a dozen little yellow Splenda packets.

Caswell watched her bite into a scone. He couldn't help notice that she was an attractive woman about his own age. Round face, prominent cheeks and eyebrows, a breezy manner born of self-confidence. Sexy too, in an offhand way. When she spoke her Mexican accent was light and fluty. He realized that he very much wanted to please her, make the interview a success. He also realized that the impulse reminded him of his teenage self, easily dazzled by feminine beauty. He grabbed the only other chair in the tiny room and sat down.

The woman sipped her coffee and rolled up the sleeves of her yellow blouse. She reached across her desk and shook Caswell's hand.

"I'm Carina Espinal. I work for Telezonda, and I understand you might like to work for them too."

Caswell waved toward the photo murals. "I've never been to San Miguel. Could be fun."

"Why head south?"

"Adventure. I'm stale, life is going nowhere, and I need a change."

"How's your Spanish?"

"Almost non-existent. *"Uno mas . . . hasta . . . ¿dónde está el baño?"*

"Well, that is a little *tacha* right off the top."

Caswell cringed. "I hear that San Miguel is full of American expats. Shouldn't be too tough to get around."

Espinal looked him over. "True. We employ some, you'll meet others. What we need are English speakers who bring some expertise or talent to our company. What have you got to offer?"

Caswell pointed a finger at his head. "I have a good mind for facts. Facts of all kinds. A few years ago I was even a *Jeopardy!* champion.

Espinal's eyebrows bounced up. "Really."

"Well, for three shows. I'm not in the hall of fame."

Espinal opened a file drawer and dug around inside.

"Here we are. We use scripts" — she waved a piece of paper — "and I have this. I'm going to read some statements, and you name the references. Ready?"

"Fire away."

Espinal cleared her throat. "Largest inland body of water in Mexico?"

"Lake Chapala."

"Correct."

Caswell grinned. "Ha! The last time anyone tried that clue Bill Murray had the answer in *Groundhog Day."*

Espinal sat back. "Yes, I remember."

She paused to gauge her potential new hire. Age about thirty-five, regular features, medium height, medium weight, possible military, not fazed by her standard process. What in hell is this *gringo guapo* doing here?

"Large lake where potatoes originate."

"Titicaca."

"Location?"

"Border of Bolivia and Peru."

"Altitude?"

"Twelve thousand five hundred feet."

"In meters?"

"Um, thirty-eight hundred."

"The Tanana is a tributary of this river."

Caswell was momentarily stumped. He was about to guess the Amazon, but then he slammed a fist on the arm of his chair. "Oh no you don't. Trick question. Sounds south, but it's way up north — the Yukon."

Espinal grinned. "Very good. Now try this . . . European city first to duplicate Chinese porcelain."

"Meissen, in Germany."

Espinal tossed out a half dozen more random statements and questions, all with obscure answers, and Caswell nailed each one. She was impressed.

"All right, champ, who is the Spanish Prisoner?"

"Some nobleman willing to reward his rescuer. It's a confidence game."

"Right."

"Or a play by David Mamet."

Espinal blinked. "Hmm, I didn't know that."

"That's okay, not his best, and I've never seen it."

Espinal consulted her script. "Tell me about the Nigerian Prince."

"Another scam. A wealthy official needs your help transferring money. Just a little cash to oil the wheels, but your promised reward doesn't actually turn up."

"Sephora gift card?"

"A friend's niece loves Sephora cosmetics. An email claims his internet is down, please buy a gift card for her birthday, pay you later. But your friend's email has been hijacked, and money does not actually buy anyone a card."

Espinal returned the script to its file drawer. She folded her hands. She didn't quite understand why this guy wanted the job, but she realized she was glad he did.

"You're pretty good at this. You might work out."

Caswell was puzzled by the last sequence of questions. "What is it with the scams?"

"Telezonda is a telemarketing company. We sell products to anyone who picks up our calls. You may be helpful designing campaigns. We want to be sure you know what's legit and what is not."

"I get it. But why me? Why anyone, for that matter? Why not AI tricks?"

"We need people who can step in when AI stumbles. Have an instinct for people's dreams, their habits, possible weaknesses."

Caswell grimaced.

Espinal cocked her head. "You'll be a well-paid salesman. Does that bother you?"

"No, no. I'm excited. Just one thing. You speak perfect American English."

Espinal smiled. "UCLA. But when I'm at home *hablo muy rápido así ¿ves?*"

Suddenly her Spanish took on the musical tones of every Mexican Caswell had ever heard speak.

She handed him an airline ticket. "Aeromexico. Someone will pick you up outside the gate."

34

CASWELL EXAMINED HIS TICKET. He had traveled to Mexico on a few occasions in the past. Cabo, Mazatlan, and Cancún on vacations; the famous *Museo Nacional de Antropología* in the big city and Teotihuacan on a tour back in his college days.

AEROMEXICO AIRLINES
SFO 14:30 -> MEX 20:10 Boeing 737 Max 8
MEX 23:15 -> QRO 00:19 Embraer 190

He was scheduled nonstop to Mexico City before continuing on a regional jet to Querétaro, the closest airport to San Miguel. The times listed included a three-hour layover in the city, arrival after midnight at QRO, and that meant a long dark drive to his final destination. Why so late? Oh right, middle Mexico observed the Central Time Zone, two hours ahead of San Francisco. He was exhausted just from thinking about the trip.

Yet here he was — four hours in the air; then dinner in Mexico City's airport; staring at Spanish language book covers in the newsstands; boarding a much smaller jet hours later; collecting his bags at Querétaro's ultramodern airport; then standing outside under the stars on a warm night, waiting for the promised pickup.

SUVs the size of yachts came and went, but none stopped for him. He checked his watch every five minutes. Five checks later a yellow Volkswagen Beetle weaved through thinning traffic and stopped right in front of him. He paid no attention until the driver emerged and shouted his name.

"*¡Caswell! Oye, gringo, ¡por aquí!*"

A dark-haired woman was thumping the roof of her car.

"Holy crap. Carina Espinal? What are you doing here?"

She laughed. "I don't recruit all the time. You just filled my quota. Jump in, it's an hour and a half to your hotel."

Caswell was dozing off the moment they left the airport. Half an hour later he felt an elbow in his ribs.

"What?"

"I've booked you into the Villa Santa Monica. It's a nice hotel and not too pricey. Stay a couple nights, but start looking for somewhere to rent."

"Santa Monica. Rent a room . . ."

The strange intimacy of a long drive late at night led Espinal to offer some advice.

"Or a house. Depending. How long do you think you'll last down here?"

"Hard to tell. If things work out, I'll give it a year."

"Definitely a house. And a separate mail box. And don't tell anyone at Telezonda where you live."

Caswell rubbed the sleep out of his eyes. "Why not?"

"Rumors have the cartels moving in. We've got something like 10,000 Americans living here, and we see them preyed upon."

"Oh? I can take care of myself."

Espinal hesitated to elaborate her warning. But after a long silence and long kilometers on the road she decided to explain.

"Telezonda itself may be falling under cartel influence. *Así que ten cuidado, ¿de acuerdo?*"

"English?"

"Watch yourself."

▼

Hotel lights were blazing when Espinal brought her yellow *vocho* to a halt in front of the Villa Santa Monica gate. Caswell collected his bags from under the hood. She handed him a slip of paper.

"Telezonda address. Southwest from here." She gave him a cool once-over. "Can you ride a motorcycle?"

Caswell pretended to grip a pair of handlebars.

"I can learn."

"Rent a bike. Parking is hell on our narrow little streets."

She waved good night and motored away.

35

A ONE KILOMETER TAXI RIDE carried Skip Caswell through a maze of narrow cobblestone streets tightly bounded by low stucco buildings painted in festive reds, yellows, and blues. He had slept late on his first day in San Miguel, he was only half-awake, and the unfamiliar shape of the small city, so old and unlike anything north of the border, had him completely befuddled.

Suddenly the cab emerged onto Salida A Celaya, a modern four-lane boulevard that could have been located anywhere in northern California, except for the Spanish signage on the buildings. The abrupt leap from past to future jarred Caswell, made him feel like a time machine's passenger.

Now he paid close attention while the cab traveled several tree-lined blocks past modest taquerías, dry goods stores, automobile body shops, art galleries, plus a vast home-grown version of Walmart, and deposited him at his new place of employment. This was a renovated stone building whose doors were shadowed within the arches of a handsome portico. Caswell noted the Spanish colonial architecture and the contrasting neon sign above the second floor windows shouting *Telezonda Global.*

"Mr. Caswell. Welcome," said Carina Espinal, rushing forward to greet him. On this morning she was wearing black slacks and a tailored black jacket.

Caswell grinned. "Look at you, *Señora,* very corporate today."

Espinal stiffened. "As you see."

She took Caswell's hand and guided him across the building's well-lit lobby to an older man wearing jeans and a *Cruz Azul* soccer jersey that would look more at home on a teenager.

"Skip Caswell, Feliciano Duarte. Felix, this is the former *Jeopardy!* champ I told you about. Skip, this is our team manager."

Duarte tipped wire-rimmed glasses down onto his nose and shook Caswell's hand.

"Good to meet you, *Señor.* Team manager — *sí* — that means you'll be working for me."

Indeed.

Duarte escorted Caswell into a large hall where dozens of tiny booths were set out in three rows, each equipped with a computer terminal, a multi-line telephone with a headset and microphone, an office chair, and padded baffles at head height to isolate each booth from all the others. He indicated the nearest chair and invited Caswell to sit. Caswell sat.

"Feels like a voting booth. My new home, I guess, huh?"

Duarte didn't reply. He fetched a loose leaf binder from the tiny desk under the computer monitor, opened it, and handed it over.

"Let us say you are selling a product to a reluctant prospect who does not hang up on you. Prospect says, not interested. You reply — what?"

Caswell felt lost. "I'm not sure."

"You do not have to be sure — we use scripts. They will govern your response. All here in this manual. Read, *diga me.* "

Caswell studied the binder page Duarte had opened.

"Um, on prospect first negative expression, say *'before we say goodbye, would you like to know more?'*"

"*Sí,* " said Duarte.

"Then if prospect expresses a second negative, say *'perhaps my offer sounds too expensive.'*"

"*Bueno.* "

"If a third negative, say *'let me show you something less costly.'*"

"Go on . . ."

"And if that leads to a fourth negative, say 'thank you for considering my offer. Goodbye.'"

"Exactly, you have it."

Caswell scratched his head. "Doe this actually work? It seems so low-key. Where's the hard sell?"

Duarte smiled, revealing a gold incisor tooth. "It does work. Statistically, it works in one-point-eight-five percent of our calls."

"That all? Geez."

"An excellent number, believe me. We have tried more aggressive approaches, but statistically they are much worse, only one-point-one percent of our calls get results with those methods."

"Okay, who am I to argue?"

Duarte flipped pages to a different section of the manual.

"I am starting you out on our campaign selling vacations in Tucson Arizona to residents of Minnesota."

"Timeshares. The worst. You have American clients?"

Duarte registered Caswell's frown of distaste.

"We have many. Most of our business is done in *el norte.*" Duarte pointed to a virtual button on the booth's computer screen. "Press this to start a call. Experienced operators keep two or three going at all times."

▼

Caswell made thirty-two calls on his first day. He sold nothing. He extended his stay in the beautiful Villa Santa Monica hotel.

On his second day Caswell made a sale. A retired professor and his wife decided that the town of Hibbing Minnesota was practically arctic and bit hard. Caswell was astonished.

At the end of his first week Caswell had sold nineteen timeshares in Tucson. He extended his stay in the Villa Santa Monica for a second week.

36

CARINA ESPINAL approached Feliciano Duarte at his desk in the Telezonda war room. She pointed at Skip Caswell, manning station number three in Row One.

"*¡Hola!* Felix. How's my recruit doing? It's been two weeks."

Duarte rubbed his balding head. "Well, Carina, you picked up an oddity. This *gringo loco* has made thirty-five sales since he started. Don't ask me how he does it, our scripts mean nothing to him. Fucking timeshares in fucking Tucson yet."

"Thirty-five sales? Is that good or bad?"

"Is good. Very good. Pete Ebersole, previously my best, sold twenty-nine when he was on that campaign."

Espinal was persuaded.

"*Luego.*"

She strolled across the room and tapped Caswell on his shoulder.

"Hey you, got time for lunch?"

Caswell spun around in his seat. He pulled one ear free from his headset. "Hello there, haven't seen you for a while. What's up?"

"Lunch?"

"I've got a fish on the line. Five minutes to my break." He paused, speculating about the sudden attention. "Then, food, okay, let's do it."

▼

They settled at a table on the patio of La Frontera, the nicest restaurant within ten blocks of the office. The eatery was not on the standard Telezonda employee rotation, and the menu offered some items with American overtones, which she thought Caswell would like.

Instead he ordered the chile cheese sweet potato and a bottle of Negra Modelo. She opted for a chicken enchilada with green salsa and a margarita.

They clicked glasses.

"So, have you found a place to stay?"

"I'm still at the hotel. It's gorgeous, the fountain, the books, the bar . . . I feel like *The Mark of Zorro* when I walk through the halls."

Espinal frowned. "I thought I told you to get out of there."

"What's the problem? I can afford it."

"Not the point."

"Well, I have been looking. I've got my eye on a house just up the road, a block off the boulevard."

Espinal sat back in alarm. "No, no, no, too close, Skip."

Caswell's turn to frown. "What's the problem? What am I missing?"

"Did you rent a bike?"

"Yeah, it's parked outside the office."

"The little red Honda?"

"Yeah, not much more than a Vespa, but all I can handle."

Espinal toyed with her margarita. How to explain?

"You can't rent near the office. If someone tails you, you'd never shake them off in that short distance. You need to start looking up north — Guadaloupe, Nuevo Progreso. Back streets, where a bike can lose anyone."

Caswell felt his skin grow cold. Clearly this woman knew something about life in San Miguel, at Telezonda Global, that he, the newcomer, did not.

"You sound awfully paranoid. *Diga me.*"

Espinal tilted her head. "Nothing, probably. You're not in California. Think. Keep your head up."

"Good advice. I'll take it."

Espinal finished her margarita. "What I want to hear."

Caswell pushed his plate aside. "Now a question for you — I'm selling timeshares over in my little cubby. But I see two more rows of booths, fully occupied. What are they selling?"

"I don't know. You'll have to ask Felix."

"Felix? *El jefe's* a silent movie. Another question — I understand a man named Horacio Monserrat is a part owner of Telezonda. You meet him? Ever see him around?"

Espinal blanched. *"¡Dios mío!* Where did you hear that name?"

Caswell gave Espinal a sideways glance. "Aha! The cartels getting a grip. That's who you're worried about. The man is dirty, but I want to meet him. I've got a job for him up north."

"What kind of job?"

"He's a movie stuntman. I need a stunt."

Espinal shook her head. "All I will say is, stay away from that guy."

▼

After lunch Caswell turned to Pete Ebersole, three booths down the row from his own location.

"Hey, Pete, how you doing?"

Ebersole pulled his headset free. "Could be better, I'm selling ergonomic pillows to side sleepers in Texas."

"Any luck?"

"I have sold eleven pillows this week."

"Ouch."

"Yeah, well, I love my work."

Ebersole had lived in San Miguel since he retired from Ernst & Young, the big American accounting firm. Caswell surmised that the old man was well acquainted with the pitfalls of expat life.

"I'm curious," said Caswell. "Here we are in Row One. You've been over there, what are they selling in rows Two and Three?"

Ebersole shook his head. "Dreams. Lucky breaks."

Caswell puffed out his cheeks. "You mean scams."

Ebersole glanced around the room to be sure they weren't attracting attention. "You said it, not me."

"You think the cartels have a stake in Telezonda?"

"Possibly. You and I would never know."

"Felix? Would he know?"

"Maybe. Ask him."

"I might."

Ebersole turned halfway back to his equipment. "Ever notice the supermarket tabloids — *'Jesus Christ Was An Alien'?* You don't think readers really believe that crap, do you? No, they just want to experience, for a moment, the feeling that crazy ideas are true."

Caswell squinted at the thought.

"Scams are like that," continued Ebersole, "the victims know they're being taken, they just want to experience, for a moment, the feeling that life is on the upswing."

"I dunno, Pete. Is that what you tell yourself?"

Ebersole adjusted his headset. "Yes. It helps."

Caswell returned to his own booth with his mind in a whirl. First Espinal's oblique advice. Now Ebersole's evident guilt. He could feel a malign cartel influence creeping up on him, like an afternoon shadow advancing across the room.

"*¡Oye! gringo* man."

Felix Duarte was beckoning.

"Carina likes you. I think you are not playing by our book, but I like you too, so I promote you. Row Two."

Caswell followed Duarte across the hall and sat down in the nearest empty chair. The team manager handed him a workbook.

"Here, as representatives of Visa, we ask prospects for their credit card information so we can hand them a big payoff from a disputed charge, ¿captas?"

"You don't actually hand them anything."

Duarte grinned. "You are quick. Instead we use the card to pad a special account of our own."

"The Standard Card Trick, sometimes called the Master Magic Trick."

"You have heard of this." Duarte was surprised.

"Sure, it's a classic. What's our success rate?"

Duarte waved a dismissive hand. "A little under one percent. Make many calls."

Caswell spent the rest of the day pretending to deposit money in gullible Americans' credit card accounts. He was not happy with the results, so he spent the next day trying an alternative plan.

As his shift ended, he armwaved Duarte over to hear his report.

"Hot news, Felix. I followed the book for a day — success rate zero-point-five or maybe worse. Actually, I only got two credit cards into our system. So I thought, we're shooting too high; it raises suspicions. Why not go for small beans? So now I spent today telling prospects there was a five dollar overcharge. And I actually paid that into their accounts."

"You did not."

"Of course I did. I paid out forty-five bucks, and then used the cards I gathered to majorly feather our special nest. The marks won't find out for weeks. My success rate? eight-point-five percent. Pretty good, wouldn't you say?"

The team manager was actually impressed enough to mention it. "*Sí,* that is not too bad."

As the news traveled through Row Two, the Standard Card Trick was abandoned by all in favor of Caswell's New Card Trick.

37

WHEN ESPINAL ARRIVED at Telezonda in the morning, Horacio Monserrat was waiting at her desk.

"*Hola*, sweetheart. *¿Qué tal?*"

Espinal regarded the handsome stuntman with wary courtesy. "I am not your *cariño*, Harry. I am your *gerente de oficina*."

"Ah, but you could be."

"You know better. For reasons you will never understand, my *corazón* is a stone. There. Just think of me as your loving *hermana*."

Monserrat chuckled. He was used to the unvarying give-and-take with his most valuable employee. He clocked her suppressed irritation without concern, filing it way with her current hair style.

Espinal rapped her fingers on the arm of her chair. "Where have you been, anyway?"

Monserrat waved a hand around. "Hermosillo. Business, like here, but heavy duty, you know?"

"I don't want to know. So, catching up — while you were away we ran into a couple of problems. Our lease is up for renewal, renegotiating our unbelievable phone bill with the Americans has stalled, and you need to sign some checks."

"Sounds routine. *"¡Bueno!"*

Espinal motioned toward the war room.

"On the bright side, I hired a new guy, and he has already added a play to our playbook. Want to meet him?"

"Lead the way."

Espinal located Caswell in the fifth booth of Row Two. He was in the middle of a hectic conversation with a widow in Boston, and his tight focus on the latest prospect did not allow for interruptions. Espinal waved a hand in front of his face to get his attention. He jumped in his seat and whipped around to face whoever dared to annoy him. He ripped his headset off.

"Carina! What the fuck? I had this woman. Had her, I tell you, and now . . ."

"Easy, Skip. There are more fish to be fried. I want you to meet one of our owners."

Monserrat stepped out from behind his office manager, hand outstretched. Caswell stood up. It took each of them a few seconds to overcome their mutual surprise.

"Skip Caswell," said Monserrat, recovering smoothly, "Well, how about you? A scambot down here doing battle in my Mexico shop."

"Harry — finally — the man I was hoping to see."

"And here I am."

"Here you are."

Monserrat grasped Caswell's hand and gave it a firm shake.

Espinal looked from one to the other. She was completely confused. "You two know each other? How is that?"

"Stunt work on a TV commercial."

"Friend of the producer."

Espinal understood that she was an outsider in some unknown situation originating up north. Her ears started to burn as she realized how and why Caswell had tricked her into getting his new job. She gritted her teeth waiting for the volcanic eruption she thought was coming from Monserrat.

But no. Monserrat laughed and slapped Caswell on the back.

"How's Sally?" he asked.

"She likes her insurance company," affirmed Caswell, "and her ransom notes."

"Yeah, that was some con we pulled. I bailed her out of a very leaky boat."

Caswell nodded. "Glad you did. She's a good woman."

Espinal heard the talk devolving into banal platitudes and picked up an unwanted feeling.

"I've got work to do, fellas. Sounds like you two fraternity brothers have some catching up to do."

She whirled away and marched herself out of the room.

Monserrat watched her go. When she was out of sight he gave Caswell a friendly jab on his chest.

"You didn't come all the way down to San Miguel to work for me. What's up?"

"Well, I kind of did. I needed a change, get a job, stop living off my bank accounts. And you know what? I'm having fun. I figured out a scam variation that's making us a lot of jack." He gestured toward his fellow agents. "Everyone's using it now."

"So I hear."

Caswell's mouth turned up in a sardonic grin. "But you aren't interested in my workplace triumphs."

"Now that you mention it. But we can't talk here."

Caswell looked around at his fellow employees. No one was paying them the slightest attention.

"No problemo, Harry, they're too busy trying to beat my totals to bother us."

"Maybe, maybe not. Let's take this outside."

Under the building's portico, where words would be disguised by traffic on the boulevard, Monserrat leaned against a pillar and folded his arms. *"Diga me* — what really brought you all the way down here from San Francisco? Make your story a good one."

Caswell waved a hand. "All right — I need a hit. And you are hard to find these days."

Monserrat looked around to be sure they were alone.

"What makes you think —"

"— Byron airport? Walter Lewis explained it all."

Monserrat paced a circle around the pillar he'd been leaning against. He flexed his fingers while he marshaled his thoughts. "Walt didn't show you the way for free, I hope. How much did he cost you?"

"Five-K."

"That fuck. How did you find Walt? He doesn't advertise."

"I made friends at a law firm catering to high tech. Rogers & Rubenstein, know them? I'm guessing not all their clients are high tech startups."

Monserrat chuckled. "No, they're not." He wondered about Caswell. The man was too young, too eager, and too upper class to be fully aware of the dirt in the bag of dirty tricks Monserrat himself practiced.

"Let's suppose," speculated the stuntman, "just as an exercise, that I help you out in my other capacity. Who's your target?"

Caswell raised a finger. "One, my stepmother is keeping me from my share of the family fortune." He raised another finger. "Two, she's got all the cards in her hand, and three, I need an ace to take over."

"Where would I find her?"

"You'd have to come back up to San Francisco. She has routines there, they take her places."

Monserrat nodded. "Okay, the States . . . fine, I could do that. Just know — I'm expensive."

Caswell sighed. "Money is always an object, but . . . whatever, I've got enough."

Monserrat slapped Caswell on the shoulder.

"I understand you are Felix Duarte's star employee. I need to think about your problem, come up with a plan. Meanwhile, keep up your good work."

When Caswell was back in his cubicle rustling money out of hopeless Americans, Monserrat took Espinal aside.

"Hey, doll, I'm not sure this new character is a good fit for us."

Espinal was not surprised to hear Monserrat's evaluation.

"No? Should I get rid of him?"

"In the nicest way possible. I think he might be a *gringo infiltrado.*"

"A spy? FBI? DEA?"

"Who knows? He doesn't add up."

▼

As the business day was winding down Espinal pulled Caswell's headset off his ears in the middle of a call and shut down his computer.

"Skip?"

"Dammit, Carina, you just vaporized another hot lead."

Espinal touched a finger to his lips.

"Hush. Listen to me very carefully. I want you to get on your bike and ride home as fast as you can. Take the back streets, wherever they are. And don't come back until I call you."

"What?"

"It might be days."

"Carina?"

"You are a moth that got your wings burned by getting too close to a cartel candle. Savvy? Now go!"

38

SKIP CASWELL HURRIED out of the Telezonda office, strapping on his motorcycle helmet in stride. Espinal watched him exit into the parking lot and moved close to a lobby window in order to see him on his bike and safely away.

Caswell mounted the Honda, kicked the starter, revved the engine, and shuffled an awkward turn toward the boulevard pavement with his heart pounding. But before he could wedge his ride into heavy afternoon traffic two Mexican men wearing sunglasses and black *Club León* jackets grabbed him and yanked him out of the saddle. The Honda fell over. One of the men ripped his helmet off and threw it into the nearby bushes. Caswell yelled for help, but none of the cars slowed down, and no one appeared from within the Telezonda building. The other man clapped a hand over Caswell's open mouth and forced an opaque black hood down over his head.

Caswell was reeling. He could feel three grainy tablets in his mouth, and he knew with terrible certainty that they must be fentanyl. If they stayed there for more than a few seconds, he knew he would be dead. With the hood in place to conceal his actions he got his tongue behind one of the pills and spit it out. Next he found the second pill and spit that out as well. He ran his tongue around his mouth, hunting for the last one, and discovered it lurking between his right cheek and a rear molar. He coughed it forward and flicked it out with heroic tongue contortions and plenty of spittle.

His vision blurred. He felt himself being thrown into the back seat of a car. He heard doors slam, and then his mind wandered away into the abyss created by the fentanyl residue.

"¡Dios mío!"

Espinal was stunned by the sudden attack. She threw open a cupboard in her desk, jerked a bulky nylon bag free, and dashed for the door.

Shielding her eyes against sunlight glaring off car windows, she strained to see into the boulevard's southbound lanes. But Caswell and his captors were well out of sight.

She threw her bag to the ground and kicked it across the parking lot. Then she stood Caswell's Honda upright, rolled it back into a parking space, and gently lowered the kickstand to hold it there.

▼

The kidnappers dropped Caswell's body in a wide dirt parking lot off the highway southwest of San Miguel. After a while, Caswell shuddered. He heaved himself onto his back half-consciously as if tossing and turning in bed. He teased the hood off his face and stared at the sky. Birds were flying overhead in loose flocks, calling to each other with musical voices. He vaguely wondered what they were. Angels, maybe? He turned his head. Over there to his right he could see a tower. He squinted and could just make out a cross topping a copper roof. Heaven? He struggled to decide the question. But thinking was too much work. His eyelids drooped, and he fell back into a drug-induced coma.

Twenty minutes later a yellow VW Beetle roared into the parking lot and screeched to a halt. Espinal leaped from the driver's seat and rushed to Caswell's crumpled form.

She pressed a knuckle hard against his upper chest. "Come on, Skip, you're not dead yet, come on, come on . . ."

She slapped his face. Once. Then twice. She grabbed his nose and twisted.

"Unghh . . ." he said.

"Skip? Hear me?"

"Unghh."

"Skip?"

His eyes closed. Espinal could tell he was slipping away. She scrabbled around in her bag.

"Where are you? Where, where — gimme that!"

Her fingers closed on a Narcan inhaler. She tore the wrapping away, rammed the nozzle into Caswell's left nostril and pressed the plunger to dispense four milligrams of Naloxone HCL.

"Unghh . . ."

"Skip — wake up!"

Caswell's head wigwagged back and forth. His eyes opened.

whooshuss

He sneezed, covering Espinal's face and blouse with strands of sticky mucus.

Espinal's lips curled. "Oh shit. Oh my God. You horrible *cochino!* Hear me, Skip? You fucking animal, wake the fuck up!"

Caswell's eyes flickered. His brows knitted together. He raised a hand and attempted to wipe away some of the goo.

"So sorry," he mumbled.

Espinal got her arms under his shoulders and, amid grunts and groans from both, levered him into a sitting position.

"Can you stand up?"

Caswell thought about the idea.

"Well?"

He bobbed his head like a puppet. "I can . . . maybe . . . with a lot of help."

▼

Espinal had her yellow VW Bug traveling eastbound along the city's border at nightfall, moving fast. Her hands gripped the steering wheel with single-minded intensity. Caswell lolled in the passenger seat, watching the scenery blur past his window.

"You found me. How the hell?" he asked as the lights of San Miguel retreated into the rear view mirror.

Espinal gave him a sidelong glance.

"They dropped you in one of two places where *all* the bodies get dropped."

"There was a church."

"Yes, *Capilla de Nuestra Consuela.* There's a useful parking lot near the steps."

"I heard birds singing."

"Lucky I tried the *capilla* first. Or we wouldn't be talking."

"A miracle," he decided. "You must be an angel."

"There's an idea."

Espinal slowed as they approached a traffic rotary and diverged from four-lane Route 111 heading east onto narrow Route 1 curving north.

"We can't drive in a straight line very far. The way it works, after an execution, killers call the cops."

"How thoughtful of them."

"Yes. Civilization must be maintained. And pretty soon after that the cops will discover your body is missing. Monserrat and his boys will be after us. So what do you think?"

Caswell didn't hear her. He was asleep again, resting his head against the VW's doorpost.

"Skip? Oh Jesus."

Espinal pulled to the side of the road where it widened into the driveway of a lonely farmhouse. She fumbled in her bag for another Narcan inhaler, stuffed the nozzle into Caswell's nose and pushed the plunger.

Back on the road Caswell woke up. His head was clearing.

"Well, hello," said Espinal. "Let me see you blink. Let me see you touch your nose with your right forefinger."

Caswell swiveled his eyes around. He blinked and touched his nose without effort.

"Looks like you'll pull through. Thank God. You had a very close call."

"Aren't you taking an awful chance?," worried Caswell. "How is Monserrat going to treat his office manager now that she's turned traitor?"

"Know what? I just quit that job."

She grinned.

"I think we can make San Luis Potosi tonight. Get ourselves into a hotel. After that we'll have to think and dodge. Think and dodge."

39

ESPINAL CRUISED past the Hotel de Lujo in downtown San Luis Potosi and parked a few hundred feet away in the Hotel Suprema lot.

"Why are we doing this?" groaned a very tired Caswell.

"My yellow *vochito* stands out. Not a good idea to show unfriendly eyes where we are staying."

The de Lujo was corporate modernity, up-to-date, clean, well-appointed, and half empty. Their room featured two queen beds. They each fell on one without undressing or turning down the covers. Caswell was asleep when his head touched the pillow. Espinal dimmed the lights and kept a silent vigil until she was satisfied his breathing was strong and regular.

As morning light filtered into the room around the edges of its blackout curtain Caswell, looking well rested, tiptoed to Espinal's bedside. She was still fast asleep. He gazed at her olive-toned face half buried in her pillow. He brushed a skein of dark hair away from her exposed ear and snapped a finger. She sat up with a yawn.

"Bathroom's yours. I made coffee. Breakfast in the lobby."

▼

After gassing up in the city, Espinal pointed her VW northward.

"We can make the border in one more day. The question is, which crossing will Monserrat be watching?"

"Let's just get there fast," said Caswell. "How about Laredo?"

"We could try," allowed Espinal, "but the cartels are well established there. Monserrat will make inquiries. It's dangerous to sprint."

"Okay, then where?"

"I think Piedras Negras. It's farther away, and maybe it will seem too far to the friends we left behind."

Caswell waved a hand at the passing landscape of sand, tussocks of dry grass, and scraggly bushes. "Since I know zip about Mexican road trips, I second the motion."

After an hour and a half on narrow back roads made of sharp curves and potholes, they reached Moctezuma on Route 12 and stopped at a grim Oxxo *gasolinera* for a bathroom break.

On returning to the car Espinal hesitated before opening the driver side door.

"You awake? Stay that way?"

Caswell was already in the passenger seat. "You bet, let's go."

"Then you should drive."

They switched places, crossing in front of the VW where they raised arms to slap encouraging high fives. As Caswell's hand fell back to his side it brushed against Espinal's. He felt his breath catch. Static electricity . . ?

▼

Two hundred and fifty kilometers south, in San Miguel, Harry Monserrat gathered his trusted cartel associates in the Telezonda offices. They were drinking beer.

"Where is my girl Carina?" he demanded.

"*¡Sí!* Where is that bitch of a whore?" echoed Felix Duarte.

"And where is she taking the American?"

The assembled men eyed each other, sharing doubts with their glances.

"They will be over the border before we can find them," declared Luiz Garza, one of Caswell's kidnappers. "Unless."

"Unless what, Lou?" frowned Monserrat.

"There is a Sinaloa guy I have heard of from my cousin, who can track telephones."

Duarte snorted. "Sadly for us, we can't do that."

"Bribe Telmex?"

"No, no — we can buy from this guy."

Monserrat was annoyed. "Buy from fucking Sinaloa?"

"I think we must."

Monserrat thought about the cost and the humiliation.

"Okay, we buy," he growled. "Track them both."

The afternoon wore on, and Caswell and Espinal switched driving duty again at a Pemex *gasolinera* just beyond San Tiburcio on lonely, dusty, Mexico Federal Highway 54.

Now Espinal was at the wheel, and Caswell was free to gaze at her while she held a steady northbound course. He was aware of a subtle tension growing between them as the kilometers rolled away beneath their wheels.

"I'm looking at you too," said Espinal with a grin.

Caswell pulled his phone, miraculously left behind by his kidnappers, from a pocket. He fired it up and started searching through his map app.

"There's a nice hotel not too far up the road in Concepción. Shall I book us?"

Espinal brushed a hand across Caswell's unshaved cheek. "I don't believe in fate, but I think maybe the *capilla* protected you. Why you're still alive and still have your phone," she said.

Then she blanched. "Oh my God, your phone. You're using it."

"Yeah, I've got a number, Hotel de Oro, what do you say?"

"Shit! Turn it off! *¡En chinga!*"

Caswell did as instructed. "Okay, we'll be walk-ins."

"Phones — they may see us. Mine is off, and I thought we discussed the problem."

"Maybe I wasn't paying attention to every word," said Caswell.

▼

Concepción was a gold rush town of low buildings on narrow streets wedged between steep palisades. Caswell thought it resembled the older sections of San Miguel. The Hotel de Oro was in sharp contrast, a modern structure bespeaking the tourist trade, but it offered only a single king bed in the room he booked.

"Well? Can we make this work?"

Espinal leaned close and planted a shy kiss on Caswell's neck.

"Maybe so."

Her touch shot through Caswell like electricity. He turned and pulled her into a tight embrace, urging his lips against hers. Their tongues met. She got her arms over his shoulders, lifted herself off the floor, and wrapped her legs around him. He twirled her across the room and dumped her on the bed.

Clothes flew off. They were breathing in gasps.

▼

Hours later, in the cool of the evening, they strolled arm in arm through Concepción's streets to the Fonda de Mineros, where margaritas, enchiladas, and fried ice cream banished all thought of cartels and their thugs.

In the middle of the night Caswell's eyes fluttered open. He turned onto his back and laced his hands behind his head. His movements caused Espinal to stir. She wedged herself against his chest.

"You know," he said, "now that I look back, I think something was going on from the moment we met."

"I was thinking the same thing," purred Espinal. "Probably why I let you trick me into hiring you."

"You let me? Ha! You never."

"That's how I like to think about it, though."

▼

Luiz Garza was on the phone to his cousin's nephew's brother-in-law from the Sinaloa cartel. At the end of a short conversation he had a report for Harry Monserrat, whom he found in the taquería across the boulevard from Telezonda Global.

"So here's the story, Harry, what we're paying for. Yesterday afternoon, my cousin's man got a blip on the American's phone."

Monserrat put down his breakfast churro and rubbed his hands on a paper napkin. "Where? Where is our *gringo?*"

Garza ran a hand through his hair. "North of us. The news is not all good. Very few cell towers up that way, and they have him on two towers about fifty *kilómetros* apart. One says he was on Highway 54 when the tower pinged his phone, and the other says east from there, over toward the gulf."

"Heading for Monterrey? Why? Or, hey, Matamoros — there's a border crossing on the coast over there."

Garza waved a finger back and forth. "My guy is not certain. It was a faint signal, and could be it got scrambled."

"Maybe your guy doesn't have the best equipment . . ." mused Monserrat.

"Or the best contacts," added Garza. "I have this thought myself."

Monserrat drained his bottle of Mandarin Jarritos. "The Sinaloa gang has a pile of our cash, so I want our money's worth. *¿Me entiendes?*"

Garza made a casual salute. "When the American gets near a city, the signal should get stronger." He was not especially hopeful.

"Or, Sinaloa could be fucking us over, Lou — so Plan B — start calling hotels."

40

BAMBA! BAMBA! sang Espinal and Caswell, motoring through high country on a long afternoon.

> . . . *to dance La Bamba,*
> *one needs a bit of grace.*
> *a bit of grace for me, for you . . .*

The couple were riding high on their overnight discovery of an ungovernable mutual passion. They bungled the simple verses, shouted the choruses, and laughed at their ineptitude.

The desert landscape whizzing by had gradually transformed itself into promising greenery as they steadily gained altitude. Joshua trees sprouted along the highway.

Soon the terrain buckled into mountain crests. Espinal's *vocho* struggled up steep grades to a high pass where they marveled over signs warning, in dire terms, not to disturb the local butterfly population. How humane, they thought. How uniquely Mexican.

By the time the terrain flattened out again the sun was sinking into a cloud bank, and the issue of lodging arose. Now that smartphones were out of the question, Caswell was forced to decode an unfamiliar paper map.

"Monclova's the only big town we'll see today. Got some hotels. Let's give the Azul a try."

Espinal assented with a flick of her curly dark hair, still humming Richie Valens' old hit tune.

The Azul, which turned out to be a Best Western Plus hotel, was another ultramodern departure from Mexico's Spanish architectural heritage, set like a jewel amid nondescript warehouses, an Oxxo, and dubious taquerías.

At the desk, an eager young man wrote up their reservation.

"So nice to see a *paisana*. All we usually get are *Americanos.*"

"Thanks."

"May I ask about your trip? Holiday? Sales? Heading north or south? I can help guide you to your next stop."

A cool feeling crept over Espinal. She glanced at Caswell, who was studying a tourist brochure.

"Skip?"

Caswell looked up, saw her give her head an almost imperceptible shake.

"What's the matter, babe?"

Espinal bit her lip. "I can't find my credit card."

"Here, let me."

Their eyes locked on each other in silent warning. He patted his pockets.

"Oh shit, wallet's in the car," he said.

"And so is my purse, darn it," added Espinal.

They smiled at the clerk, and before they could turn away he had his phone up and was snapping their picture.

"Don't worry. Our way of keeping track of our guests," he said.

"*Bueno.* Be right back."

Caswell took Espinal's hand and led her out into the night. They were ten kilometers down the road before they could really breathe.

"That damn kid had us."

"For sure. Ha! *'My purse, darn it'* — you were good."

Espinal giggled. "I wonder how he would explain the mess if we got ourselves killed in there."

Caswell was driving, and he noticed that the city's crowded buildings were thinning out. They passed a road sign with directions to Saltillo and Monterrey.

"What's the plan?" he said. "We're almost out of town."

Espinal waved an arm around. "The very next motel, no matter what. I'm exhausted."

The VW's headlights caught a sign up ahead advertising Motel Regina. Caswell turned into the unpaved parking lot through a faded wooden arch and brought the car to a halt. The motel itself, a two-story stucco-covered lump of a building, once a hopeful yellow, declared hard times with random patches of gray paint.

Espinal pointed. "I see a couple of cars. They're open."

"I thought big cities were our best way to blend in, hide out," Caswell reminded her.

"That idea isn't working so well, is it? Someone at Telezonda is calling hotels to be on the lookout."

"Obviously."

"They can't call every hotel." Espinal considered the bleak prospect of spending a night in the Motel Regina. "Especially if they don't know it exists."

An old woman checked them in to a decent room on the second floor without incident. They discovered that the motel had a bar and made a grateful dinner out of chili rellenos and bottled beer.

▼

In the middle of the night, Espinal woke up to the sound of automobile tires crunching gravel in the motel parking lot. She disentangled herself from Caswell's sleepy embrace, eased out of bed and peeked through their front window. Below, glinting in moonlight, was a black Mercedes sedan. Two shadowy figures emerged and stood beside it, studying the building. The pair silently closed the Mercedes' doors, and with the engine purring softly, moved out of Espinal's sight toward the motel entrance underneath. She heard a polite knock. Then a bell ringing.

Espinal gave Caswell a hard shake.

"Skip, Skip — get up, get dressed, they got us."

Earlier in the evening, before they collapsed into bed, Espinal made Caswell re-park her VW at the far end of the parking lot where it's location would not give their room away. She then insisted on making a reconnaissance of the motel. There was no elevator. Just an interior stairway and two outside stairs to the second floor walkway that encircled the building, one in front and one in back.

As they were pulling on their clothes, they could hear footsteps on the walkway, followed by a knock on the room two doors down, and then a knock on the room next door.

"Oh shit. Gotta go, go, go!"

Caswell had previously determined that the rear-facing bathroom window could be pried open and was wide enough and tall enough for human passage.

Caswell did the prying and Espinal hauled herself up on the sill, just as they heard a knock on their own door. Caswell boosted her through and followed, kicking and wiggling to get his weight outside.

kablam

Their door opened with a crash. Espinal yanked on his arms and he tumbled onto the deck. She reached up and closed the window. They crouched down and shuffled halfway along the back walk, tiptoed down the stairs, and ducked under the overhang.

The bathroom window reopened. "Hey!" shouted one of the men.

Now they ran for it. Espinal headed for her VW, but whoa —

pow pow pow

— gunshots brought them to a halt. Caswell grabbed her arm.

"Let's trade," he said, and bundled them both into

the Mercedes.

As they pulled out of the parking lot, Espinal threw her car keys at the VW, where they bounced off the hood. "Fair's fair," she said.

They drove for half an hour before Caswell noticed a potential problem — no car keys. The Mercedes was equipped with a push-button engine starting system, and if he ever pressed *stop,* it would likely not restart.

They conferred on tactics. Caswell argued that the car might have a tracker hidden somewhere. Espinal checked her paper map and ordered a hundred-and-eighty degree turn to take them back into Monclova. She had discovered a Hertz agency at the downtown Hotel Hacienda.

They abandoned the Mercedes on a side street.

"Got a knife or a nail clipper?" asked Caswell.

"What?"

"Flatten the tires. Slow them down if they find the car."

Espinal handed him a ballpoint pen. Caswell used it to push open the valves on each of the Mercedes' tires and let all the air out. "There! Try following us now."

Espinal ruffled Caswell's hair. "Maybe they'll be driving my *vocho,* and we'll spot them a mile off."

Next, without risking recognition at the hotel's front desk, they rented a nice little made-in-Mexico Honda HR-V.

Caswell was curious about his good fortune. "I'm amazed those jerks left my phone and my wallet behind," he said. "I just paid for this car with a credit card I thought would be long gone."

Espinal stifled a laugh.

"Dear Skip, what you don't understand is how the cartels work with our cops. When they dump a body, valuables are left as gifts, and there's nothing like a driver's license to help the cops nail down a dead man's ID."

"Wonderful. In San Francisco we get worked up over the mayor's suspicious campaign contributions."

▼

They switched drivers at an Oxxo in Sabinas, and by early afternoon were seeing road signs for Piedras Negras, the Rio Grande, and the border crossing there. The road widened into a four lane highway. Warehouses and roadside businesses acquired a sleek and stylish polish. A red billboard on a tall pole appeared.

"Look," said Caswell, "Coca-Cola!"

They motored underneath a colossal sign for Eagle Pass mounted on an overhead gantry that spanned all four lanes. Espinal pounded the Honda's horn.

"Texas here we come!"

Caswell let her evident confidence settle in for a while. Then he offered an objection.

"I'll cross the border on my passport, which I still have, thanks to the generosity of Monserrat's crew, but you'll be stuck."

"I'll talk my way across."

"No you won't. The US border is serious shit."

"You'll see."

Caswell fell silent. A faint itch tickled his brain and unfolded into a scratchy thought.

"Whoa, babe. Are you some kind of collaborator, working for Uncle Sam in your spare time? Think that's all you need?"

Espinal eyed him with motherly sympathy.

"No, you idiot. I'm an American citizen. But you're right about one thing — I do work for Uncle Sam."

This revelation hit Caswell like a grenade. Everything he knew seemed to explode into delusional fragments and whirl away into infinity. He wanted to protest, to inquire, to demand an explanation, but he was numb, at a complete loss for words.

Espinal saw the color drain from his face. "Skip? You okay over there?"

Five kilometers later, he found his voice. "Now she tells me," he said, dropping each word like a stone.

Espinal rolled her eyes. "Don't be bitter. I shouldn't have told you at all."

▼

Espinal followed directions to the auto section of the Eagle Pass port of entry, where they joined a long line of cars waiting to cross into *el norte*.

When their turn came, a young U.S. Customs and Border Protection agent scanned Caswell's passport.

"Now you, Ma'am," requested the agent.

"I lost my passport," said Espinal.

The agent frowned. "As you may know, at this port of entry we use our new Simplified Arrival Technology. Please step out of your vehicle."

Each stood in front of a camera attached to the agent's booth for a high-tech mugshot. Within less than a minute the agent certified Caswell's citizenship, but not Espinal's.

"I'm sorry, Ma'am. I cannot allow you to proceed."

Espinal's face clouded. To cover her doubts she adopted the manners of a swaggering professional.

"Listen, kid. Not only am I a citizen, but I'm also a federal agent. Get on the horn to your supervisor, commanding officer — whoever, whatever — and tell him to write down a long number I will pass on."

The agent hesitated. He seemed confused. Caswell watched the standoff with hopeful curiosity.

"Pick up the phone!" she ordered.

The agent seemed to hear the voice of authority in her bold command. He lifted his telephone off its cradle.

"I am picking up the phone. I am making a call . . . um, Major Woolsey? I have a woman here at my station claims she is a federal employee."

Espinal politely but firmly extracted the phone from the young man's hand.

"Major? Carina Espinal here by trade, and I have a secure field tag for you. Copy? It's U-2718-6213-FA-6. Repeating — U-2718-6213-FA-6. Know that I am burned in my Mexican assignment. Please waive any paper dox and clear me for entry."

Long minutes passed. Caswell was in agonizing suspense. But then the telephone voice returned.

"Sorry about the delay, Ma'am. I am instructed to issue a challenge — *how do you like your enchiladas?*"

Espinal recited the formal reply: *"I always order green salsa."*

She handed the phone back to the border agent, who listened for a moment. "Cleared? Thank you, Sir."

Espinal sighed like a leaking balloon. Caswell paid the four dollar entrance fee.

The young agent waved Caswell and Espinal back into their car, pressed a button to raise a gate, and sent them onto the Camino Real International Bridge and onward across the Rio Grande into Texas.

▼

A quarter mile behind them, a yellow VW Beetle was parked at the end of the highway. The driver observed their exit through binoculars. His passenger made a phone call.

"Sorry, Harry, those lazy CBP bastards let Espinal and the American through customs. They're over the border, in Eagle Pass."

▼

An hour later, with Caswell driving, they were better than halfway to San Antonio. They paused at the Road Ranger service complex where US Route 57 met Interstate 35 for gas, bathrooms, and snacks. Espinal insisted on driving the final leg into the city.

Conversation was sparse. Espinal kept her eyes on the road, and Caswell stared out the passenger window.

"Your perfect English," he said at last. "Your tactical smarts. You're a spy. Where'd you come from?"

Espinal pointed into the distance. "Fair question. The Mission District in SF. Dad is a professor. One of those fiery activists."

"Here's my worry," he continued. "The cartels have connections. Will they come after us, you think?"

Espinal grunted dismissively. "Cheer up. In a country famous for guns, guns, and more guns, we're as safe here as anyone else."

"Yeah, so reassuring. Makes me so happy."

Espinal left the interstate at San Antonio's Cesar Chavez Boulevard. She worked their HR-V through traffic, crossed the famous River Walk, and continued into the heart of the city, where she parked in the Greyhound bus terminal lot.

"Out you get," she said, "this is it, my friend."

Caswell came around the car and opened the driver side door.

"What about you?"

Espinal stood up and pulled Caswell into a fierce hug.

"I've got things to do here in town." She planted a kiss on his cheek and dropped back into the car. She closed the door.

"Hey!"

She rolled down her window.

"We had quite a time together," she said. "It was great. Every minute."

"You're leaving me here?" Caswell was dumbfounded.

"Get on a bus to anywhere except California and the Bay Area. I recommend Salt Lake before you turn west. That will confuse anyone out to get you."

"Wait a minute, how do I know —"

Espinal raised her hand, palm out, to forestall any questions.

"— You don't know. Here's what I want you to understand. Okay?"

"Yeah, well, *diga me . . .*"

"I'm a spook. And you will never see me again."

With that she backed the Honda around, gave Caswell a nostalgic wave, and drove off into the city.

Part FIVE

41

JOURNAL:

Here I am, back in the States.

Not in my house, however. I remember what's-her-name, the spy, and her safe house blather, so I'm renting for a while, just in case. Still on Lombard, a few doors down the street.

Mexican chapter is closed. I never think of that woman, unless at least thirty seconds have elapsed. What a dunce I turned out to be.

I considered buying a gun. Inspector Yao took me out to the SFPD pistol range by Lake Merced, and I fired off a few rounds. Then, judging by my clumsiness, he decided the most likely person to get shot would be myself, so ixnay on that idea.

Waiting to hear if Yao can restart an investigation. Lot of meat on the fire now — Monserrat of course, and also the people who took my money to pass me down the hitter trail. Maybe snare Rogers & Rubenstein. Wouldn't that be something?

Note to self: in future avoid buses at all costs.

Late on a clear fall day Caswell met Yao at their customary spot in Washington Square Park, lattes for both in hand.

"Any news?"

"Nothing you want to hear."

"Damn, this could be so big."

"Well, if The Magneto — Monserrat? — succeeds in killing you, then we might make an arrest."

"Comforting to know. What about the Butterfields? They're behind the whole thing."

Yao shook his head. "As I may have mentioned at one time or another, it all comes down to proof, Skip. Proof. And of that precious commodity we have none. Zip."

Caswell sat down on the nearest bench and sipped his coffee.

Yao sat down beside him. "I know you worked hard down there. Work doesn't always pay off."

Caswell wasn't buying. "Monserrat agreed to knock off my stepmother. Then he and his friends tried to kill me. What more do we need?"

Yao had lost patience trying to explain the legalities, but not his sympathy for Caswell's evident gloom.

"Tell me about your spy. You mentioned getting rescued by a spy down there in San Miguel, but you didn't say the spy was a woman."

"Woman? I overlooked that detail, yes I did. And you guessed how?"

"The way you look — depressed, like you just got dumped by a good-looking *chica.*"

"Think so?"

Caswell was surprised by Yao's observation and alert enough to be grateful for his friendly curiosity.

"Okay, confession. I thought we had something going, but nope. The lady has moved on. I'm over it."

"You don't sound like you're over anything."

"Give me five more minutes. And indict that slimy Magneto while you're at it."

▼

Randal Butterfield, VectorSafe CEO, and his son Hobie, the company CFO, hopped the Tiburon ferry to Angel Island on San Francisco Bay, where they were now cycling around the perimeter road on mountain bikes. Although the weekend was cold they were warmed by their exertions. They paused on the southeast point to loosen their down jackets, drink some Tailwind Endurance Fuel, and talk business. Each word spoken froze in the air as a puff of breath.

"We've got ourselves a situation, Hobie. Let's think it through. Our hitter. He did his job. Murder. And you hired him."

"Yeah, but everything was handled anonymously, long chain of go-betweens."

"But he knows your name, why you paid for a hit."

"Sure, he had to."

"Well, son, that's dangerous."

"How so?"

"You could, theoretically, blackmail him. Get paid not to give him away to the police."

"Come on, Dad, then you and I go down too."

"Maybe he isn't so sure about that. Maybe he's worried about you denying involvement. There's no paper trail. Who could prove you were the instigator?"

"Game over, Dad. Why are we even talking about this?"

"Because he might decide to hit *you,* eliminate a possibly dangerous witness. Wake up, for God's sake."

"I think you're thinking too hard. Let's ride, getting cold out here."

They remounted their bikes and continued on their tour. But Dad wasn't finished with his agenda.

"If we don't take action, Hobie, you could become the dead man who tells no tales."

"Thanks for the thought, Dad. Shift onto your granny wheel, there's a hill coming up."

42

MONSERRAT HELD COURT with his criminal associates in the Telezonda Global offices to discuss their risky situation and plan their next move.

"By now, that bitch Espinal and her American boyfriend are back in the States, who knows where," said the occasional stuntman, laying out the problem. "Depending on who they talk to, any one of the fucking US alphabets could decide to indict me, maybe extradite me like they did the Guzmán kid. We have to do something about them."

Feliciano Duarte made a fist and pointed a finger to simulate a gun. "Pow," he said. "Hunt them down?"

Monserrat wasn't too sure. "I know Caswell lives in San Francisco. But Espinal? She could be anywhere."

Luiz Garza was impatient. "I have been thinking about our office manager. She claimed to come from Jalisco, but I didn't hear the accent, the Nahuatl words. Now I think maybe she was a plant, a *gringo* spy."

"Looking for evidence against our marketing operation," said Duarte. "Makes sense."

"Another thing, Harry" continued Garza. "The guy who hired you, we need to keep him quiet. He's our biggest danger, potential leak like a fire hose."

Monserrat bounced a fist against his lips. "I have to be careful about showing up Stateside. But you're right about that business school moron who needed my services."

▼

A few days later Hobie Butterfield got a phone call. "Hello, VectorSafe Technology? Recognize my voice?"

Butterfield was flummoxed at first. He checked the Recent Calls screen on his phone and noted the country code — 52 — for Mexico. Oh boy . . .

"Magneto?"

"That's right."

Butterfield was instantly on full panic alert.

"Why are you calling me?"

"Unfinished business."

"No, no, we're done. Finito. Over and out."

Monserrat chuckled. "Not quite, Hobie." He paused. "Call you Hobie?"

"Whatever, man. Just don't call me again, okay?"

"Hang on and listen up — I need a final payment."

"Whoa there, mission accomplished. You performed your specialty, and I paid for it. You don't need anything."

"That was cash for services rendered. Now it's insurance. I want a cashier's check for one thousand dollars made out to my handle, The Magneto."

"What are you talking about? That would leave a paper trail wider than the Interstate. Put me at risk.

"Exactly. But that check will go into my bank where I'm at risk of a subpoena, just like you. It ties us together, makes sure we both keep our mouths shut."

Butterfield's nerves were vibrating. He felt helpless, and he resented being bulldozed.

"You never told me about this. I never agreed to this."

"No, think of it as a hidden bonus. When you're ready to party, I'll meet you at the Byron airport."

"Fuck that," snarled Butterfield. He was boiling hot under the collar and trying in vain to sound calm and cordial. "Wait, okay, son of a bitch — Byron airport — See you there."

43

THE TAMBOURINE RESTAURANT had a table booked for
Bella Caswell as a neutral site for another round of family business
with her recalcitrant stepson.

When Skip Caswell arrived at noon wearing a gruesome Day
of the Dead hoodie and jeans, he found his stepmother already
there with a glass of red wine at her elbow.

She gestured toward the nearest empty chair. "Here, sit, I
ordered a bottle."

She filled his glass and clicked hers against his. *"À ta santé,"*
she said.

"Cheers. I have to apologize," he replied. "I was rude last time
we got together."

Bella gave him a wry smile. "Really. I thought that was your
everyday behavior, since I've never seen anything kinder."

"Ouch."

He reached into a pocket and withdrew a small box. As he lifted
it free Robert Caswell Senior arrived in a well-cut blazer and silk
tie. He slipped into a vacant chair.

"Halloo, Skip, whatcha got there?"

"Hi, Dad. Something for Bella."

He handed the box to his stepmother.

"Open it."

She did and discovered a diamond-encrusted bracelet flashing
amethyst stones the size of M&Ms. She gasped.

"Here, let me."

Skip stood up, walked around the table, and fastened the
bracelet on her right wrist. He then leaned over and coaxed her
into a warm embrace. She raised her arm and twisted the bracelet

this way and that to catch the light. "Diamonds and my birth stones. Well, I never," she said.

Dad was startled by the gift. "Are the diamonds real?"

Skip opened his mouth to snap off a retort, but Bella got there first.

"Robert Butthead Caswell, what a terrible thing to say."

"Well, are they? I'm wondering because our son here is a relative pauper wasting his youth on internet bullshit."

"Caswell patted his father's arm. "It's okay, Dad, I'm not exactly starving."

"No, but you could be *fuck-all rich.*"

A waiter appeared to take three orders of Dungeness crab.

Bella served her husband a slug of wine. They brought their glasses together. "Here's to family."

Skip offered a perfunctory smile. "I'll second that, provided we come to an honest understanding today."

Bella beamed. "Oh we might. But first I want to hear about Mexico."

Dad brightened up. "Find a girl down there?"

Skip winced. "Nope, *nada.* But I did find the man who killed Elo, and almost got killed myself. The cops won't extradite or prosecute, however — my word not good enough. And . . . I did get acquainted with an American spy."

"You're kidding."

"The genuine article. Don't be surprised if a Mexican marketing company called Telezonda shows up in *The Chronicle* when the authorities move in."

Lunch arrived, and all three tucked napkins under their chins and dug in.

"Too bad Caswell Urban Properties doesn't own anything down that way," ventured Dad. "You could run them."

This speculative comment abruptly cooled the atmosphere and brought the meeting to its true purpose.

"You can't recruit me, Dad, I'm no businessman. I want out. On what Jay, my lawyer and financial advisor, would call *equitable terms.*"

Dad laid his fork aside and threw his napkin on the table. "Bella offered you ten mill. And you rejected it. That sounds like it's on the generous side of *equitable* to me."

Bella looked closely at Skip. "Reconsidering, dear?"

Skip required a while to formulate his thoughts. "Look at my side," he finally began. "I'm not cut out for real estate, screwing all our vendors and tenants, worried about leases; but I am your offspring, by nature and by marriage. I value you guys — love sound too corny? — and I want to feel like I'm part of the family no matter what. So it's like this — don't screw your son."

Dad sat back in his chair. He leaned toward Skip and stared at him with cool contempt.

Bella put up a hand to prevent him from making a mistake. "Skip, darling, what does Jay think qualifies as equitable?"

"He knows, and now I know, that the family is rolling in dough. You want a number, try twenty million."

Dad almost exploded. "What? You're out of your mind!"

Skip was expecting the blast. "Twenty mill and I'll go away except on birthdays and holidays."

Dad registered Skip's rejoinder with an ironic twist of his lips, noted the defiant tone with approval. He seemed to relax. He chuckled. "Category: social relations, and here's the clue, *Jeopardy!* wise guy — an exam meant to separate whim from determination."

Skip smiled. "Hey now, you're talking to the champ. What is an acid test?"

Dad reached into an inner jacket pocket and removed a sheaf of papers. He rolled them up and swatted his son with the improvised bat.

"Bella and I have conferred. Twenty it is, paid two a year for ten years." Dad dropped the papers on Skip's plate. "If you sign today, right now, in our presence."

"Got a pen?"

Skip signed in triplicate. Dad added his signature and pushed pen and papers across the table to Bella, who signed in turn. She flashed her new bangle ostentatiously while she wrote her name.

Skip gave her a wink. "Lovely bracelet, Bell. Someone told me I should be nice to you. He was right."

44

BEST BUY IN SAN FRANCISCO on a weekend afternoon. Parking lot full. Crowds in every aisle. Store sales associates impossible to find.

Hobie Butterfield was there on the edge of town, rubbing elbows with other irritated shoppers, browsing the mobile telephone section of the store. Unlike the surrounding mob, he had the foresight to make an appointment before he arrived, and finally, after a long and frustrating wait, a bright young woman wearing a Best Buy shirt pushed through the human mass.

"Hobie?"

"Yes, that's me. At last."

"You'd like to buy a cell phone. What are we talking about?"

Butterfield pointed to a variety of phones on display, each tethered to the shelf it sat on to prevent shoplifting.

"I need a couple of pay-as-you-go phones and a couple of prepaid phone cards. The dumber the better."

She pointed at the nearest instrument. "Well, here's this Alcatel Go Flip Phone." She noted his uncertainty and moved on to the next in line. "Or, how about this little Nokia? You can activate either one with a prepaid card."

Butterfield realized he had no idea what to buy. "Um, what looks good to you? Recommend something?"

The sales associate tapped the Nokia. "I like this one, it comes with a SIM card, 30 day prepaid plan, and accepts minutes from prepaid cards when your month runs out."

Butterfield picked up the phone, checked the case.

"I'll take two, please."

"Certainly."

The sales associate pulled two boxes from underneath the display and moved to her point of sale. She smiled a winning smile.

"Okay. Are you a Best Buy rewards member?"

"Think so."

"Name?"

Butterfield was momentarily distracted by the sales associate's charming grin.

"Um, Hobie."

The sales associate ran a computer query. "Here we are. I have an H. Butterfield. That you?"

"Close enough."

The sales associate made her pitch. "I can offer a ten-dollar discount on your purchase, right here at the register. Credit card?"

"I'm paying cash today."

Butterfield handed over six twenty dollar bills and accepted a five in change.

"Last thing — can you show me how to make these things talk to each other? I'm terrible with this stuff, and my nephews — that's who they're for — aren't know-it-all teenagers yet."

The sales associate hesitated.

"Well, that means activating them, and so forth. You won't be able to return them once I do it."

"Won't matter, I just need to see them at work."

She opened the boxes, inserted SIM cards, pressed buttons to get them registered on the Tracfone network, and turned them on.

"I press this button, see, and I'm looking at the number for Phone One."

She handed the other unit to Butterfield. "Here, dial me up."

Butterfield tapped the number on Phone Two's keypad, and —

ring

— Phone One responded.

"So they work in here," replied Butterfield. "Will they work out of town, in the Big Valley?"

"Oh, not to worry, Tracfones work just about everywhere. They actually piggyback on Verizon's network."

▼

Butterfield located Major Computer, a convenient electronic supply store on Howard Street within walking distance of his office. He entered the unfamiliar territory as if arriving in a foreign country.

"Help you?" asked the clerk behind the counter. He was a nerdy old man, an ex-hippie who might once have taken part in San Francisco's Summer of Love.

Butterfield had a list. "Speaker wire? Twenty-gauge uninsulated copper wire? A soldering iron and solder?"

The clerk pointed down a long aisle. "Over there."

Butterfield wandered down the aisle picking up the items. He thought he might need six feet of copper wire and found that he had to buy a hundred feet on a large spool. Oh well.

He presented his merchandise to the clerk.

"You gonna solder this stuff?"

"That's the plan.'

The clerk returned Butterfield's reel of solder.

"Go back and trade this for your tin rosin core solder You don't want to fight the wire."

Butterfield did as directed, paid in cash, gave the clerk a little salute of thanks, and walked back to his office.

▼

At the close of day, when everyone else had departed VectorSafe Technology, Butterfield locked his office door and used a small screwdriver to pry the case off one of his new phones.

It took him a few minutes to figure out which component worked as a speaker, but with the help of a YouTube video, he spotted a tiny square transducer and located its wire leads.

He heated up his soldering iron and connected a length of speaker wire to each lead, black to black, red to red.

He stripped the other end of the speaker wire and wrapped the ends around the metal prongs of a tiny LED he had liberated from a pocket flashlight. Then he dialed up the phone's number.

ring . . . ring . . . ring

The LED blinked white with each pulse of the phone's ringtone.

▼

In the morning, Butterfield drove across the bay to the VectorSafe warehouse in San Leandro. He showed his company ID badge to the security detail, deposited his keys and wallet in a plastic basket, and stepped smoothly through the metal detector.

"Good work, boys and girls," he said. "Where can I find Cliff this morning?"

The lead guard pointed. Butterfield muttered his thanks.

Cliff Holloway was the keeper of VectorSafe's military hardware. Butterfield found him at a counter fronting a pair of doors leading into a vast storage area.

"Well look who's here," said Holloway. "What's up with our CFO?"

"Fit me up for a weapon, Cliff. I have the strong desire to shoot the shit out of a big paper target."

Holloway was a stockholder. "With a picture of a nervous investor on that target, I hope."

"Damn right. Next time I have to conduct one of my show-and-tells, I want to be able to say I know our stuff works, because I have used it."

Holloway walked into the storage area and returned with an

assault rifle that was so peculiarly futuristic it looked like s science fiction movie prop.

He flipped a switch to wake the weapon up and started an app on a proprietary computer tablet that resembled an iPad.

beep

The two devices connected themselves together.

"Now let's do the whole drill."

Holloway loaded a cartridge-free round into the rifle's chamber and handed the weapon to Butterfield.

"Aim over there and pull that trigger, Hobie."

Butterfield did so.

honk

The weapon emitted a protest and refused to fire. Holloway was pleased. "See — safe as ice cream. Now let's sign you up."

He placed Butterfield's right hand, palm down, on his computer tablet's glass screen. A bright line moved steadily from one end to the other, registering Butterfield's unique palm lines and fingerprints.

"Again, aim over there and pull the trigger."

Butterfield swiveled the rifle toward a stack of straw bales and squeezed.

blamm

The rifle let fly a supersonic round that turned straw into a puff of chaff.

Holloway nodded approval. "The future looks good, Hobie. Tell that to our investors."

They bumped fists.

"Give me like, I dunno, a couple dozen rounds. I'm going to do some damage."

At the San Leandro Rifle & Pistol Range, just south of the Oakland airport, Butterfield ran a target out fifteen yards, shouldered his rifle, and blasted it with three rounds, all in the black. He then reeled the target in, detached it, folded it, and placed it in the bag containing twenty-one leftover rounds of VectorSafe cartridge-free ammo.

▼

On his way back into The City, Butterfield stopped at a Wells Fargo bank in Alameda, where he ordered up a cashier's check in the amount of one thousand dollars.

"You sure 'The Magneto' is the correct payee?" asked the teller.

"What I've been told," said Butterfield, feigning indifference. "I think it's the name on a bank account."

45

MEDIA MUSCLE was on display inside San Francisco's Stage One building when Skip Caswell arrived. Carpenters were preparing a TV commercial production, adding the final touches to a collection of small sets arranged in a semicircle, each emblematic of a different phase of someone's life. Starting on his left, Caswell observed a plausible kitchen, next a dining area, then a patio and pool, a real Ford Fusion automobile parked in a simulated driveway, and a wooden dock on an invisible lake. Off to the side he wondered at a wide and tall green screen behind an empty body harness hanging from a beam under the roof.

A production assistant saw him gawking and sidled over.

"Some operation," said Caswell. "Where can I find Sally?"

The assistant pointed to an office along Stage One's back wall.

The door to the office was open, but he knocked anyway. Inside, half a dozen members of the Spot on Spots production team were loudly griping about their problems to Sally Prudhomme. When they caught sight of Caswell, all conversation came to a halt.

"Hey, guys," said Prudhomme. "Out. All of you. I need to talk to my visitor."

The crew made their exist as one, flowing around Caswell and out the door.

"Well, hello, Skip. What brings you out today?"

Caswell lifted a shopping bag full of clothes.

"You left some stuff at my place. Thought you might want it back. Shoes, the skirt you wore at Swoopy's, a jacket, your toilet kit, and a very nice iPad.

He handed the bag to Prudhomme, who tucked it under her

desk. She tilted her head to invite a kiss. Caswell obliged with a courteous peck on her cheek.

"I got your message inviting me. I would have read it sooner, but I've been out of town."

"Having fun, I hope," said Prudhomme.

Caswell shrugged. "What are you selling today?"

Prudhomme rose from her chair. "Let me show you."

She led Caswell out to the sets, waving an arm as she described their purpose.

"We're helping DynaMed launch their new lifestyle drug, just now approved by the FDA, to treat Parkinson's disease. Our hero is going to float up in front of that green screen as if in his kitchen, twirl through the connected sets and land on the dock, where we'll have a plate from Lake Tahoe fill in the background. Then he walks toward the end of the dock and day becomes a night filled with stars. He looks up as the stars form the name of the new drug. What do you think?"

"Who's putting water in your pool?"

"Visual effects will make it look real."

"What about the new drug?"

"Panoxyzinotrib — a mouthful, huh? So DynaMed's trade name is *Starzipol.*"

Caswell made a face. "Gotta give it to that marketing team."

Prudhomme chuckled. "Terrible, right? But that's what we're stuck with."

"Name aside, is the drug any good?"

Prudhomme's jovial air vanished. "The clinical trials show that those who took the drug didn't get worse. Those who took the placebo instead did get worse. No one got better."

"And yet the FDA approved? If Dyna-something want to advertise, it must be expensive. How much?"

"I hear fifteen-hundred a month."

Caswell whistled.

Prudhomme sniffed. "Talk about bilking insurance companies. I was an amateur."

Caswell gestured toward the sets. "This production looks expensive too. You making any money?"

"We'll break even. I'm setting myself up for the big leagues. That's where the real loot lies."

Caswell looked around, feeling lost in a world he barely understood.

Prudhomme folded her arms. "Well, Dr. J . . . I've got a category and a stupid clue — why are you really here? Old lang syne?"

Caswell gave her a sardonic smile. "I'm not sure."

Prudhomme smiled back. "You mean I stumped the champ?"

"Honestly? There's always going to be a tickle, Sal. But today, now I know" — he exhaled — "I'm good as cured."

Prudhomme opened her mouth in mock surprise. She made a fist and cruised it past Caswell's head in slow motion.

"You bastard. Know what? I'm going to write up our adventures, get back to my old journalism days with the *Potrero View.*"

Caswell frowned. "Just don't tell any lies."

Prudhomme waved the warning away, pointed toward the Stage One exit, and stalked off to her office.

On his way out, Caswell crossed paths with Roger Wyecross, whose problems with VectorSafe Technology gave Caswell most of his own problems.

"Caswell? That's Skip to your friends, right?"

"Hello, Mr. Wyecross. Looking for Sally?"

"Yes I am. We have a lunch date."

"So I would have guessed. I'm also guessing you're the reason Sally's company is running in the black these days — if what I heard is true."

"I am an investor, yes. I see a big upside here, tremendous potential. She's a major talent."

"Couldn't agree more."

Upon reaching the street Caswell unwrapped a stick of bubble gum and chewed with unrelenting determination. Then he blew a big bubble and popped it.

46

ON A COLD EVENING at the southeast corner of Oakland International Airport, Hobie Butterfield ran through the pre-flight checklist on his little Robinson R44 helicopter.

He exercised the hydraulics on his pitch controls, set his carb heat on high and fired up the engine. After a minute to stabilize oil pressure, he twisted the throttle and brought the engine RPMs to 70%. He checked each of two actual magnetos separately, verified that the sprag clutch was operating, and spent the next five minutes reviewing his checklist while the engine's cylinder head temperature slowly rose. Once assured that the aircraft was ready to fly, he raised engine RPMs to 102% and lifted off.

Butterfield hovered briefly, watching his manifold vacuum gauge, and tested his machine's yaw response. Then he executed a pedal turn in place and headed east. He had a cashier's check in his backpack, an appointment to deliver it, and a grim idea in his head.

No flight plan was necessary under visual flight rules, and Butterfield had no intention of filing one. The weather was clear, visibility fifteen miles, and he found it easy to rely on the lights of freeway traffic to guide him across the East Bay cities and over the Diablo Range of hills, keeping Mount Diablo itself well to port.

Twenty minutes later he was flying over the western margin of the Big Valley, approaching tiny Byron and its little-used airport out in the flats. Before descending to land, he slowed to a hover and examined the layout from a quarter mile away. The single runway formed a long strip trending northwest to southeast, set amid a dozen hangars and utility sheds. He observed just three aircraft parked outside at the far end.

A wide area of open ground fronted the nearest structures. He vectored the Robinson north and circled around to land on a patch of grass without passing over the airport itself.

Twilight was fading.

Once the helicopter's blades stopped spinning, Butterfield grabbed a backpack out of the passenger seat and started off along the airport taxiway, concealing himself in the shadows of the hangars and darting through the openings between them.

The first airplane he came to was an old Piper Cub. Butterfield barely glanced at it. The second airplane, now seen close up, turned out to be an Air Tractor crop duster. He ignored that one as well.

The only other aircraft was a Piper Cherokee. Butterfield walked around it, inspecting. Could this be The Magneto's private plane? He didn't know the tail number and wasn't absolutely sure, but he did notice a placard on the baggage door just behind the right wing:

CLOSE AND LOCK
BAGGAGE DOOR
BEFORE FLIGHT

Perfectly normal. What made his heart beat faster was the same text repeated in Spanish:

CIERRE Y ASEGURE LA PUERTA
DEL COMPARTIMIENTO DE EQUIPAJE
ANTES DEL VUELO

He knew his hitter often traveled to and from another home in Mexico.

"Well well," he murmured.

Now he made a careful survey of the area. No one in sight in any direction, and no sound of any unseen activity.

He silently unlatched the Cherokee's engine cowling and opened it up.

He reached into his backpack for a Nokia mobile phone with connecting wires wrapped tightly around a bundle of cartridge-free assault rifle rounds. Being careful with the wires, he stuffed his homemade device into the Cherokee's engine compartment between the engine itself and the cockpit.

He relatched the cowling and presented himself in the airport office.

"Hello, Hobie," said Harry Monserrat, standing up from a McDonald's takeout dinner with Walter Lewis, the airport manager. "Got a check for me?"

Hobie dug into his backpack and handed over an envelope. Monserrat opened it, removed the check inside and gave it his careful attention.

"Wells Fargo check, your account; a thousand bucks, payable to my account; exactly as we discussed. We are square."

He reached out to shake Butterfield's hand, but Butterfield stood back, primed to offer a provocative lie.

"Listen, Harry. Take the check and go with God. But you should know I'm hearing rumors."

"What rumors?"

"A woman close to the cops. She tells me they're on to you, looking to make an arrest."

"How could that be so?"

"No idea, just what I heard. For both our sakes, you should think about getting in that plane of yours and fly your ass back to Mexico."

"My worry too," said a very nervous Lewis.

Monserrat made a fist with his thumb up. "Good advice, Hobie. Maybe I'll take it. You and your check, that's the reason I'm here at all. And now we take our business to the grave."

"To the grave," echoed Butterfield.

47

HOBIE BUTTERFIELD ZIPPED UP his jacket against a deepening chill and hiked back to his helicopter, there to await events. The more he thought about it the colder he got, and the more he was nagged by perceived flaws in his action plan.

He had found the courage to place a homemade bomb in the engine compartment of The Magneto's airplane. Congratulations on that. But the bomb was untested. Would it explode? Worse, he had not figured out how to install any hardware to cause the airplane's automatic self destruction. Detonating the bomb required a phone call. He could be freezing his ass off for hours, maybe days, before Monserrat decided to fly away.

Too late now. He nestled Mobile Phone Two from Best Buy in his lap and settled down in his helicopter's left hand seat.

Two hours later the roar of an airplane engine jerked him out of a light nap. Monserrat was sitting in the cockpit of his Piper Cherokee, having a last-minute conversation with Walter Lewis.

"Once I'm gone . . ." he shouted over the din.

"Once you're gone, you're gone," yelled Lewis. "I know what to do, don't worry about me. ¡Vámos! ¡Sal de aquí!"

Monserrat waved, buttoned up the Cherokee and taxied out onto the runway.

Butterfield gripped his primitive Nokia telephone.

"Oh my God."

He could hear but not see the Cherokee continuing to warm up at the northwestern end of the runway. After five minutes that seemed like an hour to Butterfield, the pitch of the Piper's engine rose as Monserrat pushed the throttle to the firewall and the plane began its takeoff run.

Butterfield caught sight of red and green navigation lights when the Cherokee rose into view above the airport hangars. He watched it bank toward the south, moving away, and climbing slowly into a dark sky.

"Oh man, oh man, whoa, whoa, whoa." He marked the airplane's progress, trying to guess the altitude at which his bomb might precipitate a fatal crash. Hard to be sure. He stared at Mobile Phone Two in his hand and poised shaky fingers over the keypad.

"Gotta hit it, hit it, hit it. Now, for Christ's sake," he barked, urging himself to act.

He bit his lip and typed in the number of Mobile Phone One sitting in the Cherokee's engine compartment. He pressed the call button.

BANG

Monserrat had his headphones on, listening to air traffic control in Stockton. He lurched in his seat when both of the Cherokee's engine access panels suddenly blew off in a fiery explosion, something he saw rather than heard. He tore off his headphones and was rewarded by a staccato series of lesser blasts as the remaining assault rifle cartridges ignited.

"What the fuck?"

Flames licked the engine's gas line and a bonfire erupted from each side of the airplane's nose, bathing the cabin in evil red light.

Then the engine abruptly quit, and the propeller froze at a funny angle. Now all Monserrat could hear was the crackling fire and nighttime air whistling past the windshield.

"Oh shit."

The Cherokee's nose lifted. Monserrat peered past the flames into the night landscape ahead and below. He could just make out a promising flat surface off to port and banked toward it.

"Nose down!" he shouted.

If he kept the nose down to maintain airspeed he could reach the safety of that surface, pull up, maybe execute a dead stick landing, like he learned to do years before in flight school.

"Gonna get there! Gonna make it!" he yelled. He was filled with a strange apocalyptic exuberance as he pushed the control yoke forward.

As suddenly as it started the engine fire blew out. Now Monserrat could see the flat surface ahead more clearly. He noticed it was kind of shiny in the faint light of a waning moon.

"Oh no."

The surface was flat, all right, but wasn't a fallow field or parking lot. It was the Clifton Court Forebay, a three-mile wide reservoir serving water to California's Big Valley irrigation canals.

Monserrat brought the Cherokee's nose up as he glided over the lake at a hundred knots. Without power in level flight his speed rapidly bled away. Seventy knots. Then sixty. At fifty knots the airplane stalled and plowed into the water. The landing gear caught and flipped the nose hard down into the drink. Monserrat bounced off the windshield.

He was helplessly unconscious as his plane slowly sank out of sight.

48

SALLY PRUDHOMME CALLED Skip Caswell in the morning while he was eating breakfast.

"It's on the news, Skip. Channel 4, public radio, online! Harry Monserrat — my stuntman and your boogie man — got killed last night when his airplane crashed into some irrigation lake out in the Big Valley."

"Holy crap," mumbled Caswell through a half-chewed apple fritter.

He turned on his laptop and opened up the *Sacramento Bee's* web page to check the story.

"Oh my God, it's true."

He was looking at a photograph of the reservoir where the tail plane of a Piper Cherokee was standing out of the water. Zodiacs from Tracy Fire and Rescue and motorboats from the California Department of Water Resources were clustered around the wreck. One diver was already in the water and two others were standing by. One of the boat's crew was holding the end of a long cable whose other end was out of frame. Caswell presumed that they were planning to hook the crash up to a winch back on shore and recover the mess.

"He must have drowned when his plane went under," mused Caswell, vibrating with media shock.

"I know you were after him. Now you can relax," said Prudhomme.

"I guess so, what a comeuppance, huh?" mused Caswell.

"Makes you wonder about divine retribution, doesn't it?"

Caswell's nod of agreement turned into a head shake.

"Whoops — maybe the retribution wasn't so divine. Do we

think Monserrat, an experienced pilot, knew what he was doing?"

"Um . . ."

"We do. Damn, I gotta get out there. I'll keep you posted."

▼

By the time Caswell arrived at the Clifton Court Forebay, Monserrat's Piper Cherokee had been towed across the lake and hauled onto dry land.

EMTs had erected a temporary tent canopy behind their ambulance. Monserrat's body was there on a gurney, attended by a medical examiner wearing a plastic cloak and nitrile gloves.

Cops and firemen were busy with the details of documenting the accident and securing the scene.

No one was actually guarding the wreck itself, and Caswell got himself a good look at it. He joined a fireman who was examining the ruined engine compartment.

"Half the cover thing is gone," he noticed. "Engine failure?"

The fireman gave Caswell a sour smile. "Failure? I'll say. Forensics will tag the crash being caused by a good-sized pop."

"Explosion . . ?"

"And not from the engine itself" — he pointed toward the cockpit — "look at that dent in the firewall. The big boom originated *behind* the engine."

Caswell peered into the charred compartment. "I see what you mean. Fuel leak?"

The fireman rubbed his dirty hands on a rag. "Probably."

Caswell had an alternative idea. "Or . . . was it sabotage?"

The fireman laughed. "That's a stretch. You've got an imagination, Mister."

▼

Caswell followed the ambulance carrying Monserrat's body to the Sutter Community Hospital in Tracy. On the way he made a hands-free phone call.

"Inspector Yao? Good to hear your voice. *Breaking news* — my cousin's hit man was killed last night when his plane crashed into a lake out in the Big Valley."

"Caswell? That you? What are you talking about?"

"Harry Monserrat, The Magneto, he's dead in a plane crash. It's all over the airwaves. Check your browser."

"Okaay . . . why are you calling me?"

"Because I have been looking at the wreck. The engine didn't fail, a pretty big explosion behind the engine blew the cowling off the plane and fried the thing."

"Yeah . . ?"

"The guy was a criminal, a murderer. Did he have enemies in crime land? I'm thinking yes, and I'm thinking this was sabotage."

"Could be. Any cops out there on scene?"

"Sure, all over the place, like ants. But whoa, get your butt out here — we've got a chance to tie up a big case."

"You know I sympathize, Skip . . ."

"Hey, pretend you own the case. SFPD prior jurisdiction, yada yada. The body's in Tracy. I'll bet there's interesting evidence lying around. Ask for permission or go ahead and wing it — this will be a real notch on your belt."

Yao chuckled. "Your enthusiasm for chasing shadows always amazes me. What makes you think this is such a hot potato?"

"I do have an idea. A real one. Talk to you when — if — you show the fuck up."

▼

Once Monserrat's body was secure in the hospital morgue, post-crash action shifted to Tracy police headquarters.

Caswell was waiting in the lobby with a deep personal interest in the case and no authority. For the Tracy cops, the unfortunate accident had now reached a conclusion. Nothing left but some paperwork.

But near day's end, Inspector Yao burst into the building just in time to stop Caswell from giving up on his crazy campaign.

"Well, I'll be damned," said the amateur sleuth, "you made it."

"Yeah. You told me you had a real idea. Let's hear it."

Caswell nodded sheepishly. "Sorry to be obscure, but glad you took the bait. Who had a motive to murder Monserrat?"

Yao cupped empty air with upturned hands. "Theoretically, guy like that running a criminal enterprise, maybe he owed money, maybe he hit a rival mobster. Could be anybody."

Caswell shook his head. "That's a theory, but there's one man whose future — and whose company's future — absolutely depends on Monserrat's silence. And — no surprise — that man is Hobie Butterfield, who hired him to whack my cousin Elo."

"He hired the guy, but then knocked him off? That's your idea?"

"Right. It's a good one, don't you think?"

"Seriously? Where's the opportunity?"

"Not sure. Someone told me he's a pilot like The Magneto. I do have the means, however. Did you know that VectorSafe manufactures and sells unique cartridge-free ammo for their so-called safe assault rifles?"

Yao hated getting one-upped. "I did not."

"Butterfield could have used some of that ammo to build a bomb. That airplane engine didn't quit for no reason, an explosion killed it."

"Who told you that?"

"I saw the result. Blast originated behind the engine, and the forensic team will make it official."

Caswell studied the policeman, who was still wavering. He pointed toward a locked door.

"I saw a cop go through the hall here a little while ago with a bunch of evidence bags. Use your badge — let's take a look."

Yao's badge and his false claim of an SFPD criminal investigation got the two of them into the Tracy police evidence room.

There they discovered a half-melted Nokia mobile phone.

"Possible trigger, yes?"

They also discovered a waterlogged cashier's check. The ink was runny, but still readable.

"Wells Fargo, payable to The Magneto. Easy trace."

Yao steadied his smartphone and snapped a picture.

▼

Everyone in the lobby of VectorSafe Technology fell silent at the unexpected appearance of San Francisco Police Inspector Dennis Yao and the two uniformed cops trailing him.

"We'd like to speak to Mr. Hobart Butterfield, please."

The receptionist was flustered by the police presence. "Who are you? What do you want with us?"

"Police business, Ma'am. That's all I can say."

The receptionist grimaced. "Follow me."

She led them to the elevator and up to the tenth floor, where she opened a door and waved them inside.

The VectorSafe CFO looked up from the spreadsheets cluttering his desk.

"What in the world?"

Yao stepped forward. "Hobart Butterfield? You are under arrest for the murder of Horacio Monserrat."

Butterfield's jaw sagged.

"You have the right to remain silent. Anything you say can and will be used against you in a court of law . . ."

49

THE BUTTERFIELD TRIAL was scheduled for late spring, but the high-priced lawyers hired to defend the man were granted a delay. This was the expected result of a standard tactic, but it troubled Skip Caswell all the same.

JOURNAL:

Butterfield's lawyers claimed that the damning evidence against him was, quote, "wrongly collected and preserved and disclosed." But lo and behold, judge denies the claim, and the good guys win a round. Lawyers appeal to grant bail on grounds of "family and professional ties," but judge refuses pending further investigation into Elo's death, and the bomber remains in San Francisco County Jail.

It looks like he might be there for a long time before the wheels of justice, or what passes for justice around here, turn much further.

Dad's reaction? Tears & unconditional love? Oh no. His feckless son Hobie is innocent on account of not having the balls to commit an actual murder.

And now, capitalism at work — VectorSafe Technology's stock price sank with Butterfield's arrest, and wouldn't you know it, Capital River has been able to buy at rock bottom prices, return its borrowed shares, and clear its awkward financial position at a ridiculous profit.

Even better — Rogers & Rubenstein's high-tech clients are fleeing like fairy tale rodents. Either R-&-R close their doors or pay a heavy fine or both. But lawyers, they're hard to kill, and I make no bets.

At about this time, when plum and pear blossoms were forecasting a warm spring, Skip Caswell noticed a line item in his web browser that pointed to an intriguing article in the current issue of *The New Yorker* magazine:

My Adventure Selling Short
by Azalea Prudhomme

Caswell could hardly believe his eyes. He was not a subscriber and so made a quick trip to the periodical section of his local library. There he froze in his chair as he turned the pages and an unfamiliar story unfolded. Three thousand words of clever invention mixed with self-serving distortions of the actual events and the author's role in them.

The grim reading experience left Caswell quivering with rage. When he calmed down he motored across town to Prudhomme's office in the Stage One building.

Prudhomme grinned when he showed up. "Hello there, Skip. Been a while."

"Too long, I guess," groused Caswell. "I should have stayed closer. I could have helped coach your budding literary career."

He held up *The New Yorker* magazine he snatched from the library, opened it, and slapped the offending title page.

Prudhomme gave him a wry smile. "Nothing literary going on, Skip. Just my foray into feature journalism."

"Bullshit! Want to hear the list?"

Prudhomme sensed the social fabric tearing.

"Not really. You should go. Get out of here."

Caswell couldn't stop himself. "First, no mention of payments to recruit Elo. Wyecross cast as the victim of VectorSafe fraud. Then you take credit for pegging your stuntman as Elo's hitter. And, God Almighty, you got the whole thing to unravel by charming Hobie that night at Swoopy's without a single mention of your partner's role in all of this."

"Former partner," noted Prudhomme.

"That's really low, Sal. You should be ashamed."

Prudhomme folded her arms.

"*The New Yorker* piece is what I wanted it to be — my version. A memoir. Readers love it, by the way." She waved a hand to reject all criticism. "In the grand scheme of things, who cares how accurate it is? Now I've got work to do. Go have a life."

Caswell tossed the magazine onto her desk, turned on a heel, and forced himself to leave without any more angry words.

A month later another account detailing the squalid events leading to Hobie Butterfield's indictment appeared, this one serialized in *The San Francisco Chronicle*. Skip Caswell wrote it following a farewell web gig extolling the many uses of aluminum foil in achieving personal health and safety.

JOURNAL:

I was surprised that The Chron published my take on things, since I'm not much of a reporter, and the story is already getting old. I just wanted to set the record straight, clarify what really happened.

But hey, the editors track online views, and apparently my rap is grabbing some eyeballs. Read on, San Francisco!

Looking back, I doubt that either my account or Prudhomme's has had the slightest impact on public opinion. I'm just happy knowing that Inspector Yao likes my version better.

As for Sally P., I hear that guy Wiseacre bought himself a divorce. What a shock, right? And people tell me that my so-called ex is wearing a new ring.

50

AXEL KARLSTROM boarded a Muni train at San Francisco State after a late morning class and rode the M line to Market Street. From there he hiked up Battery, then turned east on California Street. Two blocks later he was standing in front of a tiny two-story building wedged in between high rises. He observed a name, written on glass in gold leaf, identifying The Tadich Grill, San Francisco's oldest restaurant. He had been invited to please join Skip Caswell there for lunch.

Neither he nor anyone else in his family had ever dined at such a fancy establishment. He hesitated to venture inside, intimidated by the aura of money and tradition the place radiated.

"Hey, Kayo the Axe, hello?" came a voice. Skip Caswell was standing in the doorway armwaving him over.

They sat near the window at a tiny table covered by a white tablecloth as waiters in white jackets bustled around them with bread, olive oil, bubbly water, and a bottle of expensive red wine.

Karlstrom was sinking into his chair, weighed down by an ugly sense of inferiority. "What are we doing here?" he wondered.

Caswell chuckled. "You're a City native, and you ought to get to know alternatives to Chipotle."

A waiter filled their glasses.

"Try the wine — Skywalker Pinot Noir if you please."

Karlstrom sniffed at his glass uncertainly.

"Drink up. Here's to *Star Wars*, everyone's favorite fantasy."

Karlstrom forced himself to take a sip, causing his mouth to pucker. "Woof." He put down his glass. "Why the invite, old man? You need something or I'd be standing in line at the school cafeteria."

Before Caswell could explain, a waiter took their order. Mesquite broiled salmon for himself and a look of total confusion for an embarrassed Karlstrom. "Um, can I have a cheeseburger?"

Caswell shook his head. "Bring my companion the filet mignon, please, medium rare."

He opened his wallet and unfolded the printout of an obscure news story.

"All right, see this? A couple of months ago a Mexican marketing company called Telezonda Global was raided and its assets seized by the Guanajuato state government. Turns out they were operating fraudulent phone scams. I know, because I ran a couple of their scams for a while last winter."

"You did what?"

"I was on a hunt. This all went down because of that guy Butterfield, who murdered his Mexican-American hit man. Remember?"

"Maybe. Not really. I don't read newspapers very often."

"Well it was real and good riddance. What I want you to look at is this picture of the people who ran Telezonda. They're all in jail now, all except for this woman, see?"

Karlstrom squinted at a tiny low-res image. "That's a woman? I can't tell."

"She's actually an American spy. Her name when I met her was Carina Espinal."

Karlstrom grinned. "Aha! You want me to find your true love. Was she sexy?"

Caswell sat back in his chair. "Come on, Axel, with very little effort you could become an adult."

"Right. Sorry. Where is she now?"

"That is my question. Where is she? And . . . if she's still a spy, what is the name she's using these days?"

Food arrived to interrupt their discussion. They ate in silence until Karlstrom finished his filet and his shoestring potatoes.

"So this person was, or still is, a spy. CIA? Firearms? Drug enforcement? Which?"

"I don't know. She wouldn't tell me."

Karlstrom beat a hand on the tablecloth. "I dunno, old man, it's tough cracking into government computers. They all got beefed up after that North Korean attack."

Caswell produced a lopsided smile. "Maybe some did. But our government moves like a snail. I'm betting their machines are wide open to a guy like you."

Karlstrom brightened up. "How much are you betting?"

Caswell considered the question. "How about room and board for the rest of the year?"

Karlstrom weighed the offer. "Year's nearly done. Throw in next semester?"

"Okay, can do."

They touched glasses, and Karlstrom dared to try a swallow.

"I won't be able to get far without my AI connection. That okay with you?"

"Whatever works."

Karlstrom opened up his school bag and removed his laptop. "They have Wi-Fi here?"

Caswell shook his head. "Too old-fashioned. But I've got a hotspot on my phone. We can use that."

Fortified by lunch, by an apple crisp for dessert, and by a shot of amaretto liqueur, Karlstrom revved up his online contact, and while Caswell tucked into a dish of berries with Zabaglione sauce, he posed the question.

"I do not see a woman named Espinal," said the AI agent, speaking out of a heavily stylized female face.

"Show me a picture."

Karlstrom placed the tiny photo of Espinal in front of his laptop camera. Within seconds the AI agent's face disappeared and a radically enhanced version of Espinal's photo appeared on his screen.

"Does this resemble the missing person?"

Karlstrom pointed to the screen and Caswell leaned across the table to look. The resemblance was startling. "Oh my God, that's her," he whooped.

The AI agent's eyes closed. Outlines faded and reformed. Then: "I need more information. What is your purpose today?"

Karlstrom didn't really have one. "It's not me, it's this guy," he said, pointing at Caswell.

"Let me talk to him."

Karlstrom swiveled his laptop around to face his host.

"Well hello, it's Thurston Caswell," said the AI agent. "The man who wanted to know The Magneto's name."

"That's me."

"Call you Skip?"

"If that suits you . . . *Nick.*"

"You have heard the name I use."

"You told me last time, Nick — or is it Nicolette?"

"Beg pardon?"

"You're not really an AI agent, are you? No, you're that famous journalist reincarnated as the alien robot I read about, showed up around five years ago? Reputation for digging into anything anywhere you want."

Karlstrom interrupted. "Hey, what are you doing?"

Caswell raised a reassuring hand. "It's okay, we're just getting to know each other. I'm talking to Nikki Traeger, right?"

The painterly face flickered. "I can neither confirm nor deny."

Caswell touched a hand to his chest. "You know a lot about me, and I realized I know something about you — from a *Jeopardy!* clue when I was on the show."

"Looking, looking . . . yes, I see that clue," said the agent:

> Like the mermaid in the fairy tale, this creature
> longs to become human but falls short.

"You did well to understand it. Shall we proceed?"

Caswell grinned. "Please."

The face blurred, then faded from the screen, replaced by bits of decorative confetti and silently exploding asterisks. Karlstrom checked Caswell's phone to be sure the hotspot was still working. So it seemed, but many long minutes passed in uncomfortable silence while they stared stupidly at the agent's peculiar screensaver.

"Uh-oh, Skip. You blew it big time. What's with this Traeger crap?"

"I want to know who we're dealing with. What if your AI contact was Russian or Chinese? I'm trying to locate a spy, see the problem?"

"My AI agent is not Russian. Or Chinese."

Caswell shook his head. "You can't be sure, but now I am. She's a half-human robot."

"What a crock."

"So look at it this way — you have a real friend out there somewhere, not just some random bits and bytes."

Karlstrom was about to protest further when his AI agent's face reappeared.

"Hello? Sorry for the long delay. You still there?"

"Still here," chorused the men.

"Before I reveal the answer to your query," said the agent, "I need to know why you're asking."

Karlstrom sucked in his breath. "Careful, old man."

Caswell showed Karlstrom his crossed fingers.

"It's a private matter," said he.

The agent's cartoonish mouth rippled into a wavy half smile.

"That's an interesting answer. Deliberately vague, I suppose, for personal reasons?"

"Yes."

"I take that to mean romantic entanglement. True?"

"Yes again."

"Thanks for your candor. I believe your quest is innocent, and I accept your answer. Now take this down:

"Carina Espinal is the trade name of a former CIA operative stationed in Mexico, now compromised. That woman's real name is Catalina Valero, and her current trade name is Carina Durán. She is employed by the US State Department as a cultural attaché in the American consulate located in Seville, Spain."

▼

Caswell flew Delta business class from San Francisco to Madrid with a stopover in Atlanta. From there he boarded an *Alta Velocidad Española* train at Atocha Station and arrived in Seville, three hundred ninety kilometers away down south, two hours later.

Morning in the unfamiliar city magnified Caswell's jet lag, and he was relieved to discover that his room was ready at the *Hotel Inglaterra,* with breakfast available on the open-air *Terraza* high above central *Plaza Nueva.* Better yet, and confirmation of his travel agency's wise planning, the American consulate was located half a block away in the same long building.

Caswell fell asleep on his fancy king-size bed in a room so oversupplied with opulent details it made him think of the palace of Versailles.

When he woke up the sun was in the west and shadows were long.

He posted himself on a bench in the plaza with good views of his hotel and the consulate's main exit. His pre-flight inquires had already established that the office itself was on the second floor, and the only way in or out, save during a fire, was the door he was facing.

Soon after he sat down a loose group of people well-dressed for public service trickled out of that door. He kept his vigil for an hour, but the woman he still thought of as Carina Espinal did not show her face.

He wasn't surprised. The last straggler, a man about ten years his senior, was walking his way, so Caswell stood up with a question.

"American?" he asked.

"Sorry, the consulate is closed for the day. If you need help with your passport, lost and found, travel questions, I suggest coming back tomorrow. We open at ten."

"Um, no help needed, just confirming — where you came out, is that the only exit?"

The man gave Caswell a suspicious frown. "What's going on, Mister? Are you casing us?"

Caswell shook his head. "Nice evening. Sorry to bother you."

He strolled back to the hotel and a light dinner. Over a glass of tempranillo wine he reviewed his strategy. Calling the consulate and asking for *Señora Durán* — that's her trade name, he reminded himself — was an obvious possibility, but Caswell thought that might alarm his quarry and ruin his chances. He didn't dare, and so resolved himself to play a waiting game.

And the wait was a test. A long and a boring one. Each day swarms of *oficinistas* entered and exited the building. An inward flow between nine and ten, an outward flow at two for lunch, and final departures around seven-thirty, looking to be seated in restaurants when they opened, by Spanish custom, at eight.

Over the course of his stay he got to know the young man at the hotel's front desk, whose English, thankfully, was nearly perfect.

"Say, do you know if the Americans have a back door to their office?"

"No, Sir. My cousin Angela works on that floor. You must use the front door."

Sigh.

Every morning Caswell was on his bench, studying the crowds. At lunch he became especially vigilant, and on the fifth day he thought he recognized his spy.

A possible Durán was walking across the plaza, chatting amiably with an older woman. Her hair was now tinted dirty blonde in a neck-length shag haircut, and her pant suit imparted a masculine air. He groaned, realizing he had already seen her more than once without recognizing who it was.

Oh my God, she was coming his way. He turned aside in his seat, activated the camera on his smartphone, and aimed it over his shoulder to make it look like he was staring at a website while tracking Durán and her companion as they ambled toward him.

Just when they pair came abreast of his bench, Caswell stood up, turned around, and shot out an arm to intercept them.

"Carina," he said.

The two women stopped dead in their tracks. Durán brought a hand to her throat in shock. She was too surprised to speak.

"Espinal? Durán? Valero? How's Spain?"

"It's Durán," said the former spy. Her tone was emphatically nonsense free.

Caswell nodded. "I liked Espinal better, but Durán's okay."

Her companion made a questioning gesture, and Durán shooed her away.

The woman gave her a knowing smile, a discreet thumbs up, and cheerfully continued on her way to a solo lunch.

"How did you find me?"

Caswell shrugged her question away and gave himself a moment to drink in her presence. He gestured at her hair and attire.

"You're looking . . . nice," was all he could think of to say.

They stood at the proper social distance, facing each other in silence for a while, suspended outside of time, each grappling with the possible meaning of their encounter.

Then Durán bounded forward and threw her arms around Caswell. She kissed him on his cheeks, on his forehead, on his nose, and finally hard on his lips. He held on tight and whirled her around until they were both dizzy.

When at last they stopped spinning, Durán gently pried herself free and stepped back. She opened her arms out wide in the name of heaven.

"Jesus, Skip, you should've stayed away. But no, you didn't. Now this . . . this . . . this complicates everything."